IT STARTED WITH A
WINTER KISS

———

TINA BECKETT

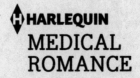

HARLEQUIN
MEDICAL
ROMANCE

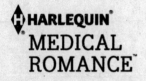

HARLEQUIN®
MEDICAL
ROMANCE™

Recycling programs
for this product may
not exist in your area.

ISBN-13: 978-1-335-14975-6

It Started with a Winter Kiss

Copyright © 2020 by Tina Beckett

Harlequin Enterprises ULC
22 Adelaide St. West, 40th Floor
Toronto, Ontario M5H 4E3, Canada
www.Harlequin.com

Printed in U.S.A.

Three-time Golden Heart® Award finalist **Tina Beckett** learned to pack her suitcases almost before she learned to read. Born to a military family, she has lived in the United States, Puerto Rico, Portugal and Brazil. In addition to traveling, Tina loves to cuddle with her pug, Alex, spend time with her family and hit the trails on her horse. Learn more about Tina from her website or friend her on Facebook.

Books by Tina Beckett

Harlequin Medical Romance

A Summer in São Paulo

One Hot Night with Dr. Cardoza

London Hospital Midwives

Miracle Baby for the Midwife

Hope Children's Hospital

The Billionaire's Christmas Wish

Hot Greek Docs

Tempted by Dr. Patera

The Doctors' Baby Miracle
One Night to Change Their Lives
The Surgeon's Surprise Baby
A Family to Heal His Heart
A Christmas Kiss with Her Ex-Army Doc
Risking It All for the Children's Doc

Visit the Author Profile page
at Harlequin.com for more titles.

To my family: for helping me follow my dreams

PROLOGUE

Fifteen years earlier

PINK-PLUS. OH, GOD.

Maura picked up the pregnancy test and brought it closer, thinking maybe she wasn't seeing it correctly. Then she closed her eyes, a wave of hope crashing through her heart as she struggled to process what had just happened. Fearing the news and yet welcoming it all the same. She was going to have a baby.

A baby!

Maybe this was the Hail Mary shot she needed to salvage her relationship with Dex and set it back on the right track. The track they had started on in high school. Until tragedy had rocked his world. And hers along with it.

He'd never been the same. Maura had

waited around, hoping against hope that once he'd had a chance to work through his grief, he would come back to her emotionally. But so far nothing had worked. He was distant. Unreachable.

Even when they made love.

And as far as grief went, he'd been strangely stoic. Even at the funeral, he'd never broken down and cried. At least not in front of her.

He needed those tears. *She* needed those tears. Just to know that he was still capable of feeling. Of loving.

And if he wasn't?

A trill of terror swept through her, and she pressed her hands to her abdomen.

Maybe she should feel him out before telling him about the baby. Or at least take a breath or two before rushing in with the news. The last thing she needed was to have him agree to stay with her for the wrong reasons.

A lifetime of living with this same unreachability? No. She couldn't do it.

She set the pregnancy test on the bathroom counter and stared at it. If he could no longer love her the way he used to, would he be able to love their child? Was she willing to risk this child growing up with a father who could not show affection?

There was only one way to find out. She needed to call and meet him to discuss things. Ask him where they stood and where he saw their relationship going.

And if he didn't give her the answer she desperately needed to hear?

Then she would have no choice but to break things off with him, give herself a few weeks to center herself and think things through. Then and only then would she figure out how to tell him he was going to be a father.

Fingering the toothbrush in a cup that sat next to hers, the one that hadn't been used since the day this baby had been conceived, she sent up a prayer that today would be the day. The day when the Dexter she knew and loved would come back to her.

God, she hoped that was possible, with every fiber of her being.

Walking from the bathroom, she found her phone on the bedside table and sank down onto her mattress. She scrolled through the list of contacts and found Dex's name among all the others. Only unlike all those other names, this one had a red heart icon next to it. He was her heart and had been from the day she'd first laid eyes on him.

And now it was up to him whether that heart remained intact or whether it splintered into a thousand pieces.

Swallowing hard, she drummed up enough courage to push the button that would either set the wheels in motion to continue their relationship or freeze them in their tracks forever.

Please, Dex, give me the answer I need.

She splayed her hand over her lower abdomen once again.

Give me the answer we both need.

CHAPTER ONE

SNOW. GREAT. HIS least favorite thing.

It came down even harder as Dexter Chamblisse exited his truck and trudged through the parking lot. He could hear the snowplow in another section of the medical center, struggling to keep the area clear enough for cars and emergency vehicles alike.

The hospital's entrance was a mere fifty feet away, but as a big flake clung to his forehead, he shoved it away with irritation. Although it never stuck around long in this part of Montana, the snow always managed to wreak havoc somewhere…for someone. About this time every year, he wondered why he stayed in this damned state. The short days and icy cold winters were always a reminder of what could happen. Of what *had* happened.

But his mom still lived here, and he felt a

responsibility to her since he was her only surviving child. And she refused to move away. He understood her reasons, but it didn't mean that Dex shared them.

Shrugging his collar up to protect the back of his neck from the fierce wind, the heel of his boot skidded on a patch of ice for a second before he righted himself. "Dammit!"

His throat tightened. All it took was a split second…

Shadowy memories slid from beneath a locked door in his brain and threatened to materialize as they'd done hundreds of times before. But not today. Not when he had a full roster of patients waiting for his help. He needed to concentrate on the living and leave the rest for another day. Preferably a day far in the future.

Stepping onto the sidewalk outside the emergency room doors, he spotted an ambulance parked in the bay with the EMTs slamming the vehicle's doors shut. He gave the one in the driver's seat a quick wave, getting a smile in return.

He wondered if *she* was on duty today and, even more, wondered why he kept entering through these doors. Maybe because he'd been doing it forever. Just because an old flame had started working at the hospital a couple of years ago didn't mean he should change his habits. Besides, it would look pretty obvious if he suddenly started using another entrance.

And it had worked out fine. As if by some unwritten agreement, he and Maura rarely ran into each other in the hospital. Even here, in the department where she worked. He had a knack for sensing when she was present, the hair at the back of his neck going up. When that happened, he moved quickly down the corridor and away, usually before he actually saw her. And when he did see her, they studiously avoided chitchat, settling for the wave of a hand as he passed through her territory.

The plan was to do the same today.

Except, once inside the ER, he found chaos.

"I don't care how many phone calls you have to make, just find me one! Now!"

He glanced to the side and saw the flash of an all-too-familiar face as she ran behind a stretcher, a tiny spatter of blood staining one of her cheeks. No more wondering if she was working today. She obviously was.

It was then that he realized his cell phone was buzzing in his pocket. A dark sense of déjà-vu slid through him, and he quickened his pace, catching up to her in a flash. Maura Findley, his ex—well, long-ago ex—had a glove-covered hand pressing on someone's chest. A boy—teenager, actually.

"What have you got?"

Her head turned, and she fixed him with a glare that spoke volumes. "Where the hell have you been, Dex? We've been trying to get ahold of you, or anyone, for that matter, for the last ten minutes."

The EMS vehicle had been carrying this patient.

Maura's tone should have taken him aback, but she'd never been one to mince words. Which was why when she'd asked him where they stood all those years ago—and he hadn't been able to give her a straight answer—she'd broken things off between them once and for all. And she'd gone on to marry someone else a year later. Hell, it had taken her almost no time to move on, something that had always bothered him. Because he'd had a damned hard time moving on with his own life.

"I just got here. Traffic slowdown because of the snow. Sorry." He tossed the word out, hoping it didn't sound like he was apologizing for their past.

He wasn't. Having that relationship end was the best thing that could have happened to him.

And her, if he was honest with himself.

He hadn't been a good catch then. And he definitely wasn't one now. Although it didn't seem like she'd made out too well with her next relationship, either. He'd heard she'd gotten divorced.

A sense of regret speared through him. One which he immediately rejected.

"We've got a penetrating chest wound with a pneumothorax—object is still embedded… traffic accident caused by the slick conditions. More are on the way."

"Holy hell!" The growled words came out before he could stop them, and she gave him a sharp look before it softened slightly. Dammit! He didn't want her sympathy, he never had.

He and Maura had been a thing in high

school—voted most likely to marry, actually. He'd agreed with them at the time. He'd even looked at rings. Planned how he would pop the question. And then the unthinkable happened and his world came apart. Their relationship continued for a while in college. But he could never get his head on straight.

Turning his attention to the kid on the stretcher, he spotted a twelve-inch piece of what looked like a galvanized pipe sticking out of the right upper quadrant of his chest. Dozens of options sped through his head. A pneumothorax was a life-threatening event if not treated quickly, and compounded by a chest wound…

"Good thing the EMTs didn't try to remove it. Let's get him into a room." He needed to be stabilized before they took him into surgery to remove the pipe.

Once in the exam room, Maura grabbed a dressing and waited for the patient to exhale before affixing the tape around the pipe to prevent more air from seeping into the patient's chest cavity.

Her hands were sure and steady, her decision to seal around the foreign body straight out of the medical books. Maura hadn't changed a bit. She was still the same mouthy, decisive girl he'd once known and loved. He gritted his teeth and sent that thought packing.

"Where are your chest tubes?"

"Third drawer on the right." She didn't even glance up as she threw the words at him, her dark ponytail falling over one shoulder as she kept working.

He used to love the natural reddish streaks in that silky hair. Loved to slide them between his thumb and index finger and…

One of the nurses came in and started getting vitals just as he found the tubing kit right where she'd said it would be. He grabbed a pair of gloves from the dispenser on the wall. "How many other victims?"

"Five or six. I'm not positive." This time she did look up. "At least one other chest wound. The weather is affecting the EMS's travel times, too."

That damned snow and ice. He couldn't think of one good thing about winter. He would rather be traipsing across places that were closer to the equator this time of the year. Places where Christmas was spent in flip-flops and colorful shirts. Maybe a trip to Brazil would be put on his agenda next year. He'd saved up enough vacation time to spend a month there. Maybe more, if he added in his personal days. Or he could volunteer with Doctors Without Borders and aim for regions in South America or Africa.

And vacation while doing that? Not very likely. But he would be able to do some good for someone other than just himself. And avoid the icy winter months and the memories that went along with them.

"His pressure is low. Blood ox in the low eighties."

Swabbing the area between the fourth and fifth ribs and placing a drape over the area, he numbed the spot with a local even though their patient was unconscious. Maura helped him elevate the head of the bed and readied a large-bore needle. "Ready?"

"Go ahead," he said.

She carefully inserted the needle into the plural space and was rewarded almost immediately with a steady hiss of air that had been trapped in his chest cavity.

"Good job."

She glanced up at him, dark eyes on his. A hint of a smile played on her lips. "I have done this a time or two, you know."

"I know. I've just never seen you in action."

Not this kind of action, anyway. And right now, he didn't need to be thinking about any other kind.

"No. You haven't." Her smile faded. Or maybe it hadn't been there in the first place. He'd been known to see only what he wanted to see. Including the fact that she'd wanted more from their relationship right at a time when he was numb to everything but the pain inside of him.

And now that the pain was more chronic than acute?

He still wanted nothing. It was easier that way. Besides, she was over him. Her marriage had proved that, even if it hadn't lasted. He shook his thoughts away from the past once and for all.

"Let's go ahead with the chest tube."

The tube would help ensure the lung stayed inflated, draining away any remaining air from the wound, as well as fluid and blood.

Maura waited as he placed the tubing in the correct position and then helped him secure it.

"That looks about as good as it's going to get," she said. "And I need to prepare for the other casualties coming in, so he's all yours."

"I'll move him into the OR to remove the pipe and assess for internal injuries." He glanced at her, the urge to brush away a tendril of hair that had fallen over her forehead coming and then going. "Call me if you need me."

Her eyes jerked toward him, and then she nodded as if realizing what he meant.

What had she thought he was referring to?

Oh, hell. They'd often said goodbye on that note after kissing each other until they couldn't breathe and then giggling over the double meaning behind the whole "if you need me" phrasing. A new sense of regret washed over him. She'd said she had something she wanted to tell him back then. Right before their relationship ended on angry words with no real sense of closure.

But there was no way to go back and fix things.

Or was there?

No. Not now when a patient's life was on the line. He'd better just accept that they'd gotten as much closure as they were ever likely to get. To try now would just rip open ugly wounds that neither of them needed to revisit.

So he gave the nurse some instructions on getting the patient to the third-floor OR and gave Maura a quick wave. The same wave he used whenever they happened to accidentally catch sight of each other. "See you later."

"Goodbye, Dex."

Goodbye.

His heart chilled. And there it was. No "see you later," or "talk to you soon." She may not have meant it to sound that way, but her meaning came through loud and clear: she had no desire to interact with him again. Now, or anytime in the near future. And he was fine with that. So, brushing her words away, he headed off to make arrangements for his patient's surgery.

Maura watched the door swing shut behind Dex, her muscles going completely limp. If not for the nurse who was still present in the room, she might have oozed into the nearest chair in order to slow her racing heart. And it wasn't just due to the burst of adrenaline from treating their patient.

God, why did she allow him to affect her like that? She'd gotten used to ducking away whenever she saw his lithe form strolling up the sidewalk toward her department as he came on duty. She wasn't sure why he insisted on coming though the ER, but it certainly wasn't because of her.

Not that she wanted it to be. Not anymore. At one point in her life, the sight of him would have made her woozy for a completely different reason. But now it was the kind of queasy awkwardness that made her cringe.

Sure, Maura, keep telling yourself that.

She was very glad her ex-husband didn't work at this hospital. Their divorce had been in part because she didn't want to move to Idaho, where he'd been offered a primo position. When she'd asked him not to go, he'd refused and walked away from their marriage instead. Looking back, it was telling that she wasn't willing to go and he wasn't willing to stay. It seemed like she had a knack for attracting men who had no desire to hang in there and stick out the tough times.

Although to be fair to Dex, he'd suffered a horrible loss during their time together. The problem wasn't that. It had come when he couldn't see past the tragedy to envision a future that honored his family's memory while continuing to live his life—making room in his heart for happiness. For starting their own little family.

Thank God she'd never needed to tell him about the baby.

Damn. She had more patients coming in, and now was not the time to dwell on things she couldn't—nor did she want to—change.

Even as she thought it, the doors to the ER swung open as the next EMS vehicle discharged a new accident victim—a girl of about ten with an obvious break to her leg, judging from the odd angle of the area below her knee.

"Let's take her back to exam room six." She glanced at Matt Foster, an EMT who was a very familiar face around these parts. "Are the rest of the victims coming to New Billings Memorial?"

He walked with the gurney, keeping his hand on the girl's arm as if to reassure her. He was wonderful with his patients, having many nurses and doctors alike asking him if he didn't want to change his career to nursing or even a doctor. But he said he loved his job. And obviously his job loved him.

This was the type of man she should be attracted to. Kind, caring and in touch with his feelings. But, unfortunately, all she felt for Matt was friendship, even though there were hints that he might like to ask her out.

"I think there's one more en route. But some of the others have been diverted to Our Lady of Mercy, since it's a little closer to where the accident happened."

So the other chest trauma case was probably going to the other hospital. A little ping of something bounced around her stomach. It wasn't disappointment. The last thing she wanted to do was see Dex again this afternoon.

Right?

Absolutely. She just needed to keep reminding herself of that fact before her brain began to put two and two together and came up with some kind of astronomical number as an answer.

She waved goodbye to Matt, who gave her a wink and a smile. "See ya later, Maura."

Turning her attention back to her patient, she said, "So what's your name?"

"Marabel Campbell." The girl sniffed, and the paleness of her features and glazed look to her eyes made Maura realize shock was setting in. It was the only reason for the child not to be screaming in pain. Hell, Maura would probably be shrieking the walls down if she'd had that kind of an injury.

"Well, Marabel, we're going to try to fix you up so you'll feel better. Is that okay?"

"Yes." She blinked a couple of times. "My mom and dad. Are they okay?"

Her heart sloshed around in her stomach before resurfacing. She hadn't thought to ask Matt about any relatives. "Let me get you settled, and then I'll ask someone."

She caught a nurse's eye. "Can you check on her parents? No one came in with her, so I don't know if…"

"I was with my aunt. My mom's at home."

"Do you know your mom's phone number?"

"My phone is in my pocket." The girl was still eerily aware of what was transpiring. Maura was shocked that Marabel, only ten years old, had a phone.

"Does your leg not hurt, Marabel?"

"My leg…" Her eyes traveled down her limbs and stopped. "No. Why is it like that?"

Torn nerves or shock could all make what should be an excruciating injury fade into the background. She had a feeling more was going on here than met the eye, though.

Just then the girl looked into her eyes. "I—I have a disease that makes me not feel things."

Not feel…

That explained a lot.

"Do you know if it's called CIP?" Congenital Insensitivity to Pain was rare, but she'd seen at least one other case during her time as an ER doctor. A man had come in complaining of nausea and sweating, only for them to discover that he was having a heart attack and hadn't been aware of any kind of pain.

"I don't know. It's a long name. But all

it means is I can't feel it when something hurts. Even when it's something like burning my hand on the stove." She turned her palm over to reveal a thick ropy scar that had probably come from a burn wound. "Can you straighten the leg out?"

The girl said it in clinical tones as if her leg weren't a part of who she was as a person. Detached.

Just like Dex and his emotions.

If anything, Maura was even more worried than she'd been before. What if the injury was worse than it looked? "We're going to do our best to make sure it's as good as new."

She took the girl's phone and pushed the icon on it that read "Mom." When a woman answered, she quickly relayed what had happened and where her daughter was.

"What? Oh, my God, I had no idea. Is Marabel okay? And my sister?"

A nurse held up a piece of paper with the name of the hospital. "She's headed to Our Lady of Mercy hospital. I'll get you that number."

"I'm on my way to where you are. Oh! And

Maribel has congenital insensitivity to pain. She can't tell if something hurts."

"Yes, she did relay that to us. It looks like she has a break to her right leg. We're getting ready to send her to X-Ray if you can give us verbal consent."

"Of course. Do whatever you need to. I'm at work, but will be there in about fifteen minutes."

"Perfect."

"Can I talk to her?"

"Yes, she's right here." She passed the phone to Marabel, who immediately burst into tears.

"My leg... What if I can't walk again, Mom? What if I can't swim?"

She wasn't sure what the woman said to her daughter, but she soon had her giggling. "Okay, I love you. I'll see you soon."

Maura already had a call in to the hospital's orthopedist, and she had the nurse contact Radiology.

Getting her young patient into an exam room, she noted her vitals, which all looked good. Maybe in part because she couldn't feel the damage to her leg. Normally blood pressure went up in reaction to stress or pain, so it was weird for her instruments not to be registering anything out of the ordinary.

Maybe Maura should have wished her own heart were a little more pain-proof and maybe she wouldn't have made some of the mistakes she had in her life.

Including not telling Dex the truth? And marrying Gabe a year later?

Probably. But pain served a very real purpose. It steered you clear of danger and taught you ways to avoid being hurt again. Like the whole stove burner thing.

So, although she might wish for a way to avoid being hurt, she needed those early-warning systems. Or she'd repeat the same mistakes of the past. And that was the last thing she wanted to do.

She immersed herself in Marabel's treatment, making sure she got what she needed, even while she gathered her own pain around her like a cloak and hoped to hell it kept everything at bay.

Like what? Dex?

Maybe. He was the only one around who could make her act stupid. Take stupid chances.

She needed to be on guard and make sure that she was well protected.

No matter how many layers of fabric she had to wrap around her heart to cushion it against future breaks. Because this time, she wasn't sure she'd be able to gather the pieces and glue them back together again.

CHAPTER TWO

Dex left the hospital eight hours later, moving across the freshly plowed parking lot. He was dead tired, but at least the snow had stopped. He passed someone bundled in a red wool coat with a matching knit cap pulled down over her ears. The person kicked her back tire, swearing in a loud voice as she did. The tire was flat. Completely flat.

He smiled even as a spear of sympathy went through him. "Need some help?"

"I'm just waiting on a tow truck. My spare's no good, either. What are the chances?"

She turned around.

Oh, damn. What were the chances, indeed?

She pulled the hat even lower as if she could hide her identity. Too late. He'd recognize that upturned nose and smattering of freckles anywhere.

He swallowed. "Maura? I thought that was you."

"Yep, although right now I'm wishing I was someone else. Anyone else."

The words hit him like a punch to the gut, which surprised him. He'd taught himself to keep most of his reactions under wraps.

His mom had often lectured him about how apathetic he seemed to be about what had happened. And she was right. But it didn't change anything. If Dex hadn't been sick enough to stay home that night… His dad had offered to wait for another night to see the movie. But they already had tickets and Dex had urged them to go without him. His mom had opted to stay at home with him while the rest of his family headed out. And look what had happened.

As if realizing how her words might have sounded, Maura cut into his thoughts. "I'm talking about the flat tire."

He relaxed slightly. "I can help you get that off and take it someplace."

"I couldn't ask—"

"You didn't. I offered." There was no way he was going to walk away and leave her here to wait in the cold. Plus, even in Montana, there were dangers such as human trafficking, and he didn't want to be responsible for abandoning her.

Sure, Dex, keep telling yourself that's the reason.

The reality was, as much as he hated it, his heart rate had shot up the second she had turned around, revealing her identity. And although he would have helped anyone—man or woman—in the same situation, this was different. It always had been. Just because his head understood that there was no longer anything between them didn't mean his body wanted to listen to reason. Or his heart.

But she sure looked cute as hell in her matching coat and hat, the big fluffy pompom on top bobbing with every sharp breeze that rolled across the parking lot. Her dark hair streamed from beneath the cap in wavy lines, and her earlobes—where tiny hoops dangled—peeked from beneath it.

"If you're sure you don't mind. How's our patient, by the way?"

"The pneumothorax? We got the pipe out

without any problems. Amazingly enough, it didn't hit anything vital."

"Wow, that's great."

"It is. He was extremely lucky." If Dex didn't know better he'd think she was stalling. "Where's your jack?"

She glanced at her trunk and grimaced. "Well, it's kind of…in there. Wait here, and I'll get it for you."

There was a tenseness to the words that put him on edge as she pushed a button on her key fob. Something released and her trunk popped open. Disregarding her words to stay where he was, he rounded the end of the car and looked down to see her trunk piled high with clear plastic packages filled with what looked like bedding. Or something. It was the same kind of knitted stuff as her hat.

Now he understood her hesitation. "What is all this?"

Her half shrug seemed irritated. "Just some things I was going to take down to a local shelter."

He fingered one of the packages, which contained a pink and blue blanket. Something tugged at him. "Did you make these?" As far as he knew, she hadn't knitted when they were together, although how would he really know? And that made something squirm inside of him. How much of their time together had been about him and his own needs?

"It's just something I do in my spare time."

Since her divorce? He didn't want to picture her sitting alone at night on her couch, making blankets for women who were even lonelier than she was. Or maybe she wasn't lonely at all. Maybe she went out with a different man every night. Or had one special someone...

Somehow that thought was even worse, so he blanked it out. "We could drop them off on the way to getting the tire fixed, since we'll have to take them out of the trunk anyway to get to the jack. Let me get my car and pull it around."

"You don't have to. Really."

"I'm off for the rest of the afternoon so it's not a big deal. I'll just be a minute."

Without giving her a chance to argue, he headed a few rows over to his car. Starting it up, he came back around to where she was parked. He opened the door to the back seat, went over and scooped up an armload of the blankets, and loaded them into his car.

She watched him for a minute, hesitating as if unsure of what she wanted to do, and then she finally started helping. "I'm sure this is the last thing you want to do with your time off."

She was wrong about it being the last thing, but it certainly wasn't the smartest thing to be doing. "I didn't have any plans so it's fine."

Not that he normally made many plans outside of work.

A few minutes later everything was unloaded, and he raised the cover in her car's trunk to find the spare. It was just a metal rim, with no tire on it at all. She was right when she said it was no good. But at least her jack and lug nut wrench were right where they should be.

In short order, he had the bolts removed and gave a tug on the wheel removing it. He loaded it in his own trunk and slammed the lid. "Ready?"

She nodded. "Thank you, again."

Opening the passenger door for her, he

waited for Maura to slide inside. "Not a problem."

At least he hoped it wouldn't be. The last time he'd been in a car with her was…

On the day they broke up. He wasn't sure what had precipitated that last showdown, but she hadn't given him any wiggle room at all. He'd known for a while she was tired of waiting for him, but all thoughts of rings and popping the question had died along with his family. And when he'd finally admitted that he didn't know what their future looked like, her eyes had watered, and she'd said they were done.

As far as he knew, she'd walked away without ever looking back at that decision. It was better if he didn't revisit that day, either. It would change nothing.

Soon they were off hospital grounds and he turned on Central Avenue heading into the heart of the city. He'd programmed the GPS for the address she'd given him. It wasn't far. Less than five miles.

"When did you start making those?" He inclined his head toward the back seat.

"Around three years ago. A friend mentioned the center, and it just seemed like something I wanted to get involved in after my…"

Her voice dropped away after that word, and she shot him a glance without saying any more. She'd only been divorced for a year, so if she'd started making the blankets three years ago, it wasn't because of that.

"I take it the ones in the car were made more recently."

"About four months. I can get two done a week under most conditions."

"That's a lot of knitting."

She glanced over at him with a smile. "Crocheting, actually."

"There's a difference?" He couldn't stop his own lips from curving. It felt good. He couldn't think of many things that made him smile anymore.

"Knitting needles are used in pairs and are straight. A crochet needle has a hook."

"Like a bone hook?"

This time she laughed. "I guess you could compare it to that, although I've never tried crocheting with one of those." She glanced out the window. "It's just a few blocks up on your right. The Nadia Ram Crisis Center for Mothers."

"Is Nadia Ram the founder?"

There was a second of hesitation. "No. Her family founded the center in her honor."

She didn't offer more than that, and a dark foreboding set up shop in his gut. Was Nadia a casualty of domestic violence? Oh, hell… Was Maura?

Pressure built in his head when he thought of someone hurting her. Physically or mentally. If that were the case, he might have to track the man down and give him a little taste of his own medicine.

"Your husband didn't… He wasn't…" He couldn't force himself to finish the sentence.

"It's *ex*-husband. And, no, he didn't." She hesitated. "I had a miscarriage years ago. It was a hard time, and I never really got over it. My friend suggested helping out at the center where there were babies and children in trouble. Nothing more than that."

She'd had a miscarriage. When? Had it been what ended her marriage? There was a depth of meaning in her last sentence that told him her involvement in the center was a lot more than "nothing." But the tension in her voice told him that further discussion on the matter wasn't welcome.

Fortunately, the GPS warned him that they were about to arrive at their destination. And sure enough, a plain brick building came into view on the right. There was no signage other than an abstract rendition of a mother holding a baby. He could understand why they wouldn't want to announce their presence, although he was pretty sure most locals would know exactly what the building was used for.

"There's a parking lot and entrance around back. That's where I normally drop off things."

"Okay." Swinging into a narrow lane that led to the rear of the building, he was surprised to see two long banks of windows and a brick patio area with chairs and picnic tables. There was also a glassed-in porch, where a young woman in jeans sat in a rocker, leaning over a wrapped object. When she lifted her head, even from this distance, he could make out two butterfly bandages on her left cheek. And one of her arms was in a navy blue sling. He swallowed hard, averting his eyes to give her privacy.

What had he expected to see? Happy faces and ladies drinking tea in fancy cups?

Maura didn't seem as taken aback, however. She waved, and as soon as the car came to a stop, she grabbed a plastic-wrapped packet from the back seat and leaped out of the vehicle. Leaving him in the car, she headed for the woman, who slid her baby into a nearby crib and opened the door for Maura. The two hugged, and Maura opened the package and held out the blanket. The woman used her good arm to shake the creation open, looking at it for a second before holding it tight to her chest. Then she hugged Maura again for a long moment. The ER doc leaned back and looked in the other woman's face, saying something. They both went over to the crib, and Maura smiled at the infant.

Her mention of a miscarriage came back to him. He hadn't heard anything about that, and normally the hospital grapevine was a wealth of information, even when the last thing he wanted to do was hear about who was dating whom.

A lot had happened since he and Maura had called it quits. At least in her life. She'd married, lost a baby, gotten a divorce and who knew what else. And she was now an ER physician. He wasn't surprised at that. They'd both talked about becoming doctors when they were dating. But in terms of anything in his own private life, things were pretty stagnant.

Stagnant. That probably wasn't the best word to describe where he was. But even if it was, that's what he'd wanted. What he still wanted. At least he hadn't given Maura or himself the additional heartache of a divorce and a lost baby.

As if hearing his thoughts, she turned to glance at him and said something to the woman. Then she opened the screen door and came back down the sidewalk toward the car. He powered down the window.

"Sorry about that. She's waiting for her parents to get here to take her and the baby home to Kalispell. I was afraid with my tire problem I'd missed saying goodbye to her."

Located in northwestern Montana, Kalispell was a good four hundred miles from

Billings. A long way to travel unless this move was to be a permanent one.

"I'm glad you made it, then."

"Thanks to you." She gave him a look that he couldn't read, and then said, "Let me go in and get a cart so I can take the blankets in and we can be on our way."

"Do you want to wait with your friend until her parents get here?"

"I just wanted to make sure she was okay and that they really were coming. The relationship has been strained over the last couple of years because of her husband. Obviously, their instincts about the man turned out to be right."

Meaning the woman's husband really had been abusive. "Damn. I hope he got what was coming to him."

"He won't. Not this time. She's not pressing charges. She just wanted out of the relationship."

So the man was free to do the same thing to another woman. The thought made more acid churn to life in his stomach. "Can't the authorities do something?"

"Not when she claims she fell off a bicycle.

They went and talked to him, but you probably know how much good that does."

He'd dealt with a few broken bones caused by domestic violence and had seen exactly what Maura was talking about. It still made him angry. But he did understand the desire just to get away and never have to face that person again, which if charges were pressed they almost certainly would.

"I've had a case here and there where I've seen the same thing." He glanced again at where the woman had gone back to holding her baby. "Did the baby have to suffer any—?"

"No, thank God. That's part of the reason for this place. It's where women can come with no pressure and no judgments. The important thing is that they left their abuser, so the emphasis is on getting them patched up both mentally and physically. Making sure they're strong enough to move forward in life."

He nodded, realizing she was still standing in the cold. Getting out of the car, he said, "Between the two of us, we should be able to carry those blankets inside. That is, if it's okay for me to go in."

Some shelters were protective about who came on the premises—with good reason—since some of these women probably suffered from PTSD symptoms.

"Thanks. It should be okay. They try to keep the residents out of the main lobby, where anyone off the streets can come in. There are separate social areas inside the facility."

Smart.

They carried the remainder of the blankets in through a back door. The person behind the desk greeted them with a smile. "Hi, Maura. Did you get to see Celia?"

"I just did. I'm glad her parents are almost here."

"So are we." The young blonde woman behind the desk shifted her gaze to him.

"Oh, sorry," said Maura. "This is Dexter Chamblisse. He's a doctor at the hospital where I work. I had a flat tire, and he offered to help drop off the afghans."

Her description of him could have been about any doctor at their hospital.

Because that's what you are, Dex. Just another doctor that she works with.

And damn if that didn't bother him on a level he'd rather not examine.

"Nice to meet you, Dr. Chamblisse." She shook his hand. "I'm Corbin."

"Call me Dex." He sent her a smile even as his peripheral vision kept careful track of Maura's movements. But she stood still, not twitching so much as a muscle.

"Thanks, I will." She glanced at the bundle in his arms. "Just set those on the desk."

They both placed the blankets on the wooden surface as Corbin oohed and aahed over several of them. "I've had people, from when you first started bringing them, contact us asking for your name. Why you won't let them send you thank-you cards is beyond me."

"Because it's not about me. It's about them. It always has been. I'm glad they seem to enjoy them, though."

"They do. Especially the baby afghans."

She made some of these for infants like the one in that closed-in patio. He remembered her saying it was because of her miscarriage. So many questions came to mind. How far along had she been? Had the child she'd carried been a boy or a girl? Why had she opted not to have another baby afterward? She'd made it clear she didn't want to talk about it, though, and he was going to respect the unspoken request.

But Dex could remember the days when he'd dreamed of having children with her. That had never happened. Nor would it.

Corbin gathered several of the blankets and slid them into what looked like a hotel laundry collection cart.

"Are there other people who make things like these, as well?" he asked.

"We have some folks who make rag quilts or stuffed animals or even kid's pillowcases. Our rooms are pretty Spartan by necessity, so it's a touch of home that can make things seem *hopeful* rather than hopeless. And it's something they can take with them as they start a new—and hopefully better—life."

"I can see how those things would be treasured." The image of the woman clutching Maura's blanket to her chest as if it were a lifeline was burned into Dex's head. It would be a long time before he forgot that.

What was he doing for anyone outside of

his job as a surgeon? Nothing. At least nothing like this. Maybe he really should start thinking about ways to give back. Like donating his services to a medical relief organization, as he'd thought about earlier.

But maybe it was time to do more than just toy with that idea. Maybe it was time to throw his hat into the ring and do what he hadn't thought to do in the past: help those who were unable to help themselves.

Dex was quiet on the way to the big-box store to see about fixing her tire. Was he regretting helping her? Or maybe the side trip to the crisis center for moms made him uncomfortable. She wouldn't blame him. It wasn't an easy thing to see a woman with a cheek that had been split open by someone who supposedly loved her. But the cuts and bruises that were inside of Celia Davis were so much worse than the wounds visible on the outside. At least her baby would be spared from witnessing her mom being beaten.

Was that what was bothering Dex?

As horrible as it sounded, she hoped that was it. Because if it wasn't…

Surely he couldn't have guessed the truth. She wasn't even sure why she had mentioned her reasons for crocheting those blankets. It had just slipped out, the way it did when anyone asked about her reasons for helping with the crisis center. She had stopped the actual words from coming out when he first asked, only to reveal it a little while later. But she hadn't explained everything, and if she could help it, she wouldn't. Not ever.

She'd been devastated when she had lost her baby, although what she should have felt was relief. But it was as if her last connection with Dex had been severed—the last reminder of what they'd once had. She'd cried for weeks, only sharing with her family and closest friends what had happened. No one at New Billings knew about her loss. There was no reason to bring it up. Not with them, and certainly not with Dex.

And there was no reason to. He hadn't asked whose baby it was. At this point, she hoped he assumed it was her ex's.

And if he didn't?

Well, she couldn't go back and change things now, and Dex had given her little choice when they were together. Maybe deep down he'd known something was up and hadn't wanted to face it…or deal with it. Maybe that's why he'd been so ambivalent about taking their relationship to the next level. And she definitely hadn't wanted him to commit for reasons other than love. But he didn't even offer.

She'd only just found out about the pregnancy herself, so there was no way he could have guessed what was up back then. And after losing his dad and siblings, something inside of him had changed. He'd made love to her a day after the accident with an intensity that had shocked her. But afterward, he'd become increasingly moody and detached, and who could blame him? As time went on, it had only gotten worse. Instead of moving back to his normal loving self, he'd become a stranger she no longer recognized.

Even after all this time, she sensed the same detached attitude in him. Having lived through it once, she wanted no part of who Dex was now.

She would just keep her secret to herself. To reveal it now wouldn't bring anything good, and it wouldn't undo what had happened.

And if she hadn't miscarried?

She would have told him about the baby. Right?

Yes. She would have. Even after their breakup, she'd formulated plans and scratched them out again. Then she'd lost the baby and there'd been no reason to.

"Everything okay?" His voice knocked her out of her musings, and she realized they had arrived at the big-box store.

"If you want to drop me and the tire off, I can call someone to come get me when it's ready."

"I don't mind waiting, unless there's a reason you'd rather I didn't."

There was one. But if she didn't kick these melancholy memories away, he was going to start asking questions she'd rather not answer and bring back memories she'd rather not face.

"Nope, I just don't want to keep you from whatever you have going on."

"Like I said earlier, I don't have any special plans, so it's not a problem."

How sad was it that neither of them seemed to have much of a social life anymore?

Well, hers was of her own choosing. She'd failed at two relationships so far and didn't relish attempting a third one. Or repeating an old one. There was a part of her that realized her marriage to Gabe had been an attempt to cover up the gaping hole left by her miscarriage and her breakup with Dex. She'd been wrong to get involved with him when she was still trying to come to terms with her own grief.

Matt Foster, the EMT, had sent little hints that she pretended not to pick up on. She didn't want to ruin their friendship by going out with him when she knew her heart wasn't in it. And using a relationship to cover up yet another hole in her life would be repeating the same mistakes. She needed to break the cycle before it became even more destructive.

They dropped off the tire and were told it would be about an hour before it was ready.

An hour. Lord, she'd hoped it would be a quick fix and that she'd be on her way in fifteen minutes. Evidently, it was not to be.

So here she was sitting in a nearby restaurant with him, trying not to look at him through the young, dewy eyes she'd had when they first met in high school. He'd been on the baseball team, and she'd sat in the stands and gawked at him game after game. And when he asked her to the prom, she'd been over the moon. He'd been so sure of himself. So sure of what he wanted. And what he'd wanted back then had been her.

She hadn't been able to get enough of him. Separating that man from the one who now sat in front of her was hard. Which was why the avoidance game at work had become so critical to being able to work at the same hospital as him.

The man was still a looker. In fact, he'd just grown more attractive over the years. With his bronzed skin and sharply cut cheekbones, he hadn't grown flabby with age. The same traits that had made her swoon back in high school were still there. As were those pale green eyes that had made her want to fall into their depths. Those eyes had been warmer back then—not the chilly pools they were today. The hardened edges of the Dex that sat across from her had crinkles radiating from the corners of those eyes, although she'd rarely seen him smile. There was also a frown line deeply etched between his brows.

It made him look forbidding. And cold.

And it also awoke a little part of her that said she could fix him. Heal him from whatever seemed to be tormenting him. But she hadn't been able to do that fifteen years ago after that tragic car accident. And she knew enough from life experience to understand that she couldn't fix him now. Dex had to heal himself.

If he even needed healing.

Maybe he was happy with the way he was, and it was her psyche that was dredging up the torment from the past. The pain she'd seen in him after the accident that had claimed everyone in his family except him and his mom.

How he'd hated the snow after that. Had avoided driving in it, if at all possible.

Did he still hate it?

She knew he drove in it, since it was pretty hard to avoid that reality in Montana.

Heavens. She was staring at him. But when she glanced quickly at his eyes, she saw he was looking out the window, not even paying attention. Probably ruing the fact that he'd offered to help her out. It had turned out to be quite a time suck for him.

"I'm really sorry this is ending up taking so long."

His attention snapped back to her. "Not a problem. I need to eat anyway, and so do you if your day was as busy as mine was."

"We were pretty hectic. Besides that big traffic accident, there were several other fender benders because of the weather this morning."

"No fatalities?"

"None that I heard of."

He nodded, his face grave. "Good."

Was he thinking about his family? She was pretty sure that was something you never got over. Maybe if she'd given him some more time…

Somehow she doubted it.

The waitress had already taken their orders, which would hopefully be here any minute. She was feeling more awkward by the minute.

"I'm sorry about your miscarriage."

His words came out of nowhere, his eyes

focused on her with an expression she couldn't decipher.

Oh, God.

A rush of tears welled up in her throat before she could stop them, and for a minute she couldn't make her voice work. She blinked, willing the flood to recede before it overflowed the levy banks she'd erected many years ago. Taking a slow, careful breath, she tried to keep her expression neutral. "It… It was a long time ago."

"But it still hurts."

"Yes." What else was there to say? There were times she could barely breathe it hurt so bad. She'd wanted that baby desperately, despite the breakup, despite the fact that she might very well have had to raise the child all by herself. What she'd done by herself, however, was face the loss of that same child. She'd lain on her bathroom floor the morning it happened and sobbed until she'd had no strength left. It had been too much. She'd lost Dex and her baby almost back-to-back.

And while those things might have happened a lifetime ago, it didn't mean the raw emotion from those events didn't rear its ugly head at times. Nor did it mean she didn't wonder what might have happened if things had been different. If Dex had been able to love her and be there for her when it happened.

But things weren't different. And they never would be.

If she was smart, she would keep that thought at the forefront of her mind. That Dex had been lost forever to her the day she'd broken it off with him. Actually it had happened before that, when his father and siblings had died in the terrible crash. The process of pulling away had been steady and inexorable, and nothing she'd done to combat it had had any effect.

There was no going back and undoing the past. For any of them. And trying would only bring more hurt and more heartache. For her. And probably for Dex, too.

CHAPTER THREE

TWO DAYS AFTER his outing with Maura, Dex awoke still feeling hungover and out of sorts.

Except he hadn't been drinking. Planting his palms on the bathroom counter, he tried to get the image of that woman—what was her name… Celia?—out of his head. He tried to imagine the fear and horror that would come from realizing the person you loved wasn't who you thought they were. Or that they'd changed over the course of a year…two years.

Which was why Maura had broken things off with him. She had suddenly realized he wasn't heading toward marriage anytime soon. Maybe never. She'd been right. But it hadn't always been that way. In his younger days—before the accident—he'd been moving steadily toward making her his partner for life. In fact he hadn't been able to imagine a universe in which they weren't together.

Somehow hearing about her miscarriage had brought it all back to him. If things had been different, that might have been *his* child she'd carried…and lost. He'd been sitting there thinking about that exact thing when they'd been in the restaurant. Even though it wasn't, it was like there was a grain of sand under his skin that just kept chafing at him. It refused to go away, no matter what he tried.

He'd just have to let it run its course. He rubbed a palm over the stubble on his face before picking up a razor and getting to work removing it. His shift started in a little over an hour. But for the first time in quite a while, he found himself sluggish and out of sorts. He'd succeeded in going almost two years, with little interaction with Maura other than a random sighting as he moved around the hospital. And that's the way he preferred it.

Yesterday had changed that—and hell if he hadn't been the one who'd initiated the contact and opted to extend it. Not a smart move. Because it was making him see things he'd been blind to at the time of their breakup.

Like the fact that in trying to protect himself, he'd probably hurt her terribly.

At the time, he'd made himself believe he was sparing her from being with someone who no longer knew how to feel. Who no longer *wanted* to feel. Because the guilt of being a survivor when he should have died along with the rest of his father and siblings had eaten at him until there'd been little left.

How could he eat, drink and be merry? How could he get married and have children knowing that he'd been spared because he'd had a sniffle and had whined that he didn't feel like going to see the movie? He'd wanted to call Maura, instead, and have a nice long chatty conversation about what they were going to do over the next couple of days.

All the while his dad and sisters had been on a collision course with death.

He hadn't been able to face it or let Maura in on that truth, so he'd blocked it out and let her walk away. He still blocked it out whenever he could.

If the universe was lining up the stars in hopes that they would force him and Maura back together, they were going to be disappointed. Neither of them wanted to travel down that road again. He dropped the razor back into his toothbrush holder and sluiced his face with warm water, washing away the last of the shaving cream.

There. He felt a little more human now.

He dried his face, slinging the towel around the back of his neck and walking back into the bedroom, where his clothes for the day were laid out on the bed.

The bed that was only rumpled on one side.

Dammit! Whether he shared his bed for a night—or not—didn't matter. What did was that he was the one who decided when and where any of those encounters occurred. And how long they lasted.

Which was almost never longer than a week or two. The women knew that up front and most seemed happy with the arrangement. At least he'd never heard any complaints. Had never been asked what his intentions were.

Maura had been the only one who'd actually stood in front of him and demanded he tell her where he saw the relationship going.

Then again, she was the only one he'd ever

had an actual relationship with. And he'd destroyed it.

Not purposely, but in the end, it had been the right thing to do. The only thing he could do.

Still, no more offering to run her places. Next time he'd wait with her until the tow truck arrived and then be on his way. No more little forays into the past. Or into the present. And definitely not into the future.

With that thought in mind, he got dressed, glancing again at his bed with a frown before straightening the covers and erasing the evidence that he'd slept alone.

Slept? Not much. But that was going to change. He'd faced the problem and dealt with it. His conscience was clear when it came to Maura and their breakup, and it would stay that way.

Even as he thought it, a little voice in his head warned him to not be too sure, because he hadn't yet seen what the day had to bring.

The day brought chaos with a capital C.

He got to the hospital and found a host of television cameras stationed outside the entrance to the Emergency Room. And news vans were parked every which way in the lot behind it. What the hell?

Swinging into one of the physician's parking places, he decided he was going to use a different entrance today to avoid whatever was going on. Then he spotted a red bobbing pompom. It was making a beeline for that mob of reporters. Great. He knew that hat. And that quick, confident walk.

Why was she heading straight into the fray?

Because Maura had never backed away from anything in her life. Except for him.

And there was probably an emergency case in there she was needed for. He had to make sure she made it inside without incident.

Before he could talk himself out of it, he exited his car and slammed the door—a little harder than necessary—moving with long strides toward her.

If he was smart, he'd just veer away and avoid whatever was going on, like he'd planned. It wasn't like the reporters were going to knock her to the ground, so he wasn't sure what he hoped to accomplish by going over to her. But all that rational thinking did nothing, because he just kept on walking.

He caught up with her within a minute.

"What's going on?"

She glanced up at him in surprise. "You haven't heard the reports?"

"What reports?"

"There was a shooting down by the moms' crisis center."

The place where they'd taken the blankets? "*By* the center? Or *at* the center?"

"At. I was about a mile out when it came across the news. I couldn't get here fast…" Her strides faltered and she cleared her throat. "I'm not sure how bad it is, but one of the center's residents was hit as she was coming out to go to work."

"Only her?"

"Yes. They suspect the husband, but he fled the scene before anyone knew what happened."

They reached the group of reporters, who waved microphones in their faces and launched a bevy of questions at them.

When someone jostled Maura, he put an arm around her waist and drew her close, forcing his way through the group. A security guard immediately came out of the door and briskly waved the reporters away from the door. He came back in with an apologetic grimace. "Sorry about that, Maura. The police are en route from the scene. Hopefully, they'll clear out those reporters."

The hospital was private property, but it was hard for one guard to force them away. "Thanks for the help."

"Where is she?" Maura glanced at the man.

The guard didn't ask who they were talking about. "Room four. They're trying to stabilize her before rushing her up to surgery. She took two bullets to the chest."

Dex felt Maura flinch against him. Room four was one of the trauma rooms.

"Who's the surgeon, do you know?"

"Dr. Hodges, I believe."

Realizing his arm had tightened around her and that she was actively leaning against him, he eased away before anyone got any ideas—especially the reporters outside, whose eyes he could feel on them. As if coming to the same conclusion, Maura jerked sideways. The guard's head tilted, but he didn't say anything.

Perfect, he'd probably made it look even worse by doing that.

"Dr. Hodges is a good trauma surgeon."

She glanced at her phone. "I know. I'm going to run back and see how she is."

Dex nodded again at the security guard. "Thanks again for your help."

"Not a problem."

Moving away from the man, he asked, "I'll come with you in case they need an extra set of hands."

"Thank you."

Just then two nurses rushed by them, one of them shoving a crash cart in front of her.

Dammit. He knew exactly where they were going. Room four.

They entered the large room, finding mass confusion and a floor littered with bloody gauze. Dr. Hodges was already inside yelling out orders to those around him. He spotted Dex. "Get in here, I need your hands."

Moving over to his colleague, he saw immediately what was wrong. An abdominal wound pulsed blood in steady, rhythmic gushes. "There's a nicked artery in here somewhere. I need to get it clamped and move her to surgery or we're going to lose her. Pressure's falling."

While Hodges worked on finding that artery, widening the hole with a scalpel, Dex worked on getting her pressure up so she didn't completely crash. Maura was against the wall somewhere, although he didn't take the time to look up. There was only room for so many doctors at a time. If he hadn't been here, he was sure Maura would be the one beside Hodges. And by how shaky her voice had been for a few moments when they'd entered the hospital, it was probably a good thing she wasn't.

Not an easy situation for anyone, but especially when it was someone you either knew or had an interest in.

"Got it. I need a clamp." A nurse passed one over and the trauma doctor sealed the vessel. "Let's get her to the OR right now. Can you scrub in?" He shot Dex a look.

"Yes. I'm right behind you."

Together they got the patient's bed moving, slamming through the doors at the end of the emergency department. He spotted Maura. "I'll let you know as soon as we know something."

The words were tossed across in a way that was totally impersonal, but it was the best he could do at the moment. He couldn't make her any promises. Something he seemed to repeat when it came to Maura. No promises. No firm commitments. But this time it was more a case of *can't* rather than *won't*. Because right now, he wasn't sure the patient was even going to make it to surgery.

Maura let one of the nurses know where she'd be and asked her to call if she was needed. She had gotten to the hospital a half hour before her shift started, just as she always did. Most of the time it gave her an opportunity to get up to speed on what was going on and gauge the feel of the ER. If there was frenetic activity, she would join in to help immediately. But on a quiet day, she'd take the time to have a coffee and get her mind where it needed to be.

She didn't recognize the shooting victim from the center, but she was young. So very young. And to have someone do this to her almost before her life had begun was unfathomable.

She hoped they caught the bastard who'd shot her. Even more than that, she prayed the girl would live to see another day. Although the center tried to stay low-key, with most of their clients finding out about them by word of mouth it wouldn't be hard for an abusive partner to discover where they'd run to.

And that was another thing. Most of the women who arrived had a child in tow or were pregnant. The center even offered child-care for those women who were working and didn't have day care arrangements.

Was there a baby or toddler at the center wondering when her mom was going to come back?

Or if she would?

The pressure that had been steadily building in her chest grew tighter, and she struggled to breathe past the constriction. She used the time to call the moms' crisis center, only to have it go straight to voice mail. They were probably dealing with the same problem with the press that the hospital was. She left her name and phone number and asked if there was anything she could do to help. She was sure they had already notified next of kin, which was strange since no one had arrived that looked like family. Maybe they were from out of town like Celia Davis's family was. One thing controlling people liked to do was isolate their partner so that they were almost completely dependent on the abuser for necessities like money, companionship and medical care. Having no place to turn to and no money even for bus fare made it that much harder to leave when things became unbearable.

Or maybe this woman's family was as dysfunctional as the rest of her life was.

Maura wrapped her arms around her waist and stared over the banks of chairs in the waiting room. It was still early enough in the morning that the surgical ward was not yet in full swing.

Just sit down. Dex said he'd let you know.

She wandered over to the nearest chair and slumped into it. It had only been about twenty minutes. If they'd lost her, surely he would have already come out to tell her. That had to be a good sign then, right?

She swallowed. The feel of his arm around her waist had been solid and comforting, like old times. Times when they'd laughed as they slipped away to a little-known creek that had been their favorite hangout spot. A place where they'd talk. Where they'd made love. Where she'd felt a sense of belonging.

Only she didn't belong. Not anymore. And once she'd realized she was relishing his closeness a little too much as they'd walked toward the hospital, she'd been horrified, especially when he tried to extricate himself, probably wondering why she was suddenly snuggled up against him.

She hadn't been. But she had been leaning against him. Needing his strength like she had back when they were together.

It had been the shock of the situation.

Her phone buzzed and she tensed, glancing at the screen. Not Dex. Although why she thought it would be, she had no idea.

It was the women's center.

"Hello? This is Maura Findley."

"Dr. Findley, this is Colleen Winters, director at the women's center. Are you at the hospital?"

"I am."

There was a pause. "Any news on Sylvia? I would have called the hospital's main number but…"

"I understand." She had to be careful how much information she gave out. "Did Sylvia make the center one of her emergency contacts?"

"Yes, I faxed it to the hospital this morning. It's one of the first things we do so that the abusive party doesn't step in and try to make medical or financial decisions for these women. It takes away a chunk of their power."

"Good. I'm relieved to hear it." She'd wondered if the man would come here, even though the police were looking for him. "Did they catch him?"

"Yes. About a block and a half away from the center." There was a long pause. "Unfortunately, he turned the gun on himself before he could be apprehended."

"He's dead?"

"Yes."

Damn. She hated that he wouldn't face justice. If she lived, that was. "Sylvia is in surgery. So far no news, but it was touch and go in the OR. Does she have family nearby?"

"No. She grew up in the foster care system until she graduated from high school."

"Wow." Somehow that made it even worse. There was nowhere for her to turn except for the shelter.

"I know. The system does the best it can, but I'm sure you know how difficult it can be to place a teenager in a permanent home."

She didn't know from experience but could imagine it would be hard.

Just then Dex came out of the back, looking wrung out and tired. And his day had only just begun. Just like hers.

"Can you hold for just a minute? I see one of the surgeons." She hit the mute button on her phone. She studied his face but couldn't read anything in it.

Just like that last day they'd been together, when his expression had revealed nothing. No frown. No tears. No surprise. Even as she was breaking off their relationship. Down by their little creek. Only that creek wasn't theirs any longer.

She waited until he reached her. "Did she make it?"

"It was touch and go, but so far she's hanging in there. We won't know for a couple of days if the severe blood loss affected her brain or other organs."

"Oh, no!"

She got back on the phone. "Does Sylvia have a child at the shelter?"

"Yes, a three-year-old boy."

Who might wind up in the foster care system, just like his mom, if she didn't survive.

"She made it through surgery, but nothing's certain right now. What will happen to her son while she recovers?"

"He'll have to go into the system, but we do have a couple of staff members who are certified as foster mothers, so it may be that he can stay here for a bit."

Dex's head tilted. He had to be wondering who she was talking to. She covered the mouthpiece. "It's the crisis center."

She finished up her call with Colleen, who said they would send someone over to be with Sylvia as soon as they had enough help to cover what needed to be covered.

Until then Sylvia was alone. In more way
than one.

Her heart ached for the young woman who
had received such a rough start in life and
for whom things had gotten no better once
she was out on her own. But if she survived,
hopefully, this would be a turning point for
her.

"Is she in ICU?"

"Yes. She's on a ventilator in a medically
induced coma at the moment. Her body needs
time to heal. We had to give her six units during the surgery to repair the artery."

"She has a three-year-old son."

Dex frowned. "Hell. Hopefully, he's not in
the care of whoever did this to her."

"No, he's not. And the shooter turned the
gun on himself before he could be arrested."

He took a step closer before stopping where
he was. "Did you know her?"

"No. So many of them come and go in
a short period of time. I've really only in-
teracted with a few of them. But the center
has asked me to teach a first-aid course over
there. I'm seriously thinking of saying yes."

"Do you think that's wise, Maura?"

She frowned at him. "Sorry? Why would there be anything wrong with educating them on—"

"There's nothing wrong with that." He held up his hands. "I meant for you. These are women who have been in unstable relationships. Violent relationships that sometimes end up with them fighting for their lives."

She still wasn't sure what he meant. "I don't follow."

"That could have been you." He took another step forward and touched her hand. The briefest brush of fingers against fingers. "What if you'd been delivering blankets today, or teaching that class?"

A shaft of something went through her. That same feeling of belonging that she'd had earlier. She shoved it aside. "It could have been anyone, including the people who work there or another resident."

"I know but..." He dragged a hand through his hair. "Hell, I need a coffee. You?"

She hesitated, but something in his demeanor told her to go with him. Maybe she wasn't the only one who'd been affected by what had happened. "That sounds wonderful. But I can't take long. I'm due in the ER."

"I'm due on rounds as well, but they'll call us if they need us."

"Okay."

They got onto the elevator around the corner and Dex stared at the ground, not saying anything. What was going on? First his concern and the touch of hands that had sent a shiver through her, and now this brooding silence.

"What are you thinking?" It was a stupid question, and one she really didn't want an answer for. But there was no taking it back now.

He was silent for a moment longer before making eye contact. "When would you teach this class?"

She blinked, then realized he was talking about the first-aid class she'd mentioned a few minutes ago. "I'm not sure. I haven't said yes yet—although I think I will—so nothing is carved in stone. Probably in the late afternoon after my shift normally gets over and when most of them would be home."

"Well, let me know. Maybe we could team teach it."

A tinge of shock made her speechless for a second. "Team teach? I don't understand."

"If you're talking late afternoon, you'd probably still be there after dark, yes?"

"Probably, why?"

"I just think it would be safer to have more than one person there."

It hit her. He was worried about her.

A rush of warmth went through her, pulsing through her veins despite all her efforts to stanch the flow. She lifted her chin, praying he wouldn't see the truth mirrored in her eyes. Forcing her voice to stay cool and even, she said, "I've been doing things on my own for a very long time now."

Since before her divorce, even, as she and Gabe had seemed to be on different pages for most of their marriage. It had held together a lot longer than she'd expected it to.

And maybe some of that had been due to laziness on both of their parts. But once he'd been offered the position in Idaho, it had forced both of them to take a good, hard look at their relationship before deciding neither of them had the energy or the desire to fight for their marriage. It had been the right decision. For both of them. Maybe the true reason for that was now standing in front of her.

God, she hoped not. Her divorce had come after she'd started working at the hospital and realized that Dex also worked there. Had that played a subconscious role in her decision not to go with Gabe?

The thought horrified her. What if it was true?

Well, at least she knew her ex-husband wasn't going to come back to track her down and try to kill her in a fit of jealous rage. Not that there was anything to be jealous of. Dex had made his thoughts about her clear fifteen years ago.

She did understand where he was coming from in not wanting her to go to the center by herself, though. And she appreciated his concern—more than she would admit. Even if it was unfounded. "Look, if you want to come and help me teach the class, that's great. But do it because you want to, not because you feel like you have to."

"I'll tell you what. Let me have a couple

of days to think something through before you give the director your answer, okay? Maybe we can offer to do a series of hospital-sanctioned seminars in different areas, like finances. Self-defense. Prenatal care. First aid. Postpartum depression. I want to ask if we have a budget for community outreach."

She hadn't thought of that. "Thank you. That sounds like a great idea. And it would be a great help to those women."

"So you'll wait?" They stepped off the elevator and headed down the hallway to the cafeteria.

"I will. It'll give me a chance to think of what I'd like to cover if I teach the class." She hesitated. "Do you think the reporters are still out front?"

"I don't know. It depends on whether they got what they wanted or whether they were run off by the police."

The coffee shop was busy, but no signs of anyone with cameras or microphones. Not that there would be. She was pretty sure the security guard would have ushered them out of the hospital corridors if he'd had his say.

"Grab a seat, and I'll get the coffee."

She glanced around and spotted a table. "Okay, thanks."

"What do you want?"

"Skinny vanilla latte. Two sweetener packets, please."

"I'll be right back."

She studied him as he waited in line. A head taller than the other folks who were there, Dex had always stood out from the crowd, and it wasn't just due to his height. It was his presence. There was just something about him.

He'd been worried about her. She could have sworn that was why he was suddenly interested in helping at the center.

And she liked it.

So very much. She leaned back in her chair. Of course she'd liked him "so very much" once upon a time, too. It's why their breakup had ripped her heart from her chest. And the fact that her baby might very well have grown up without a daddy. When she finally got up the courage to tell him about the pregnancy, she'd started cramping. And then her heart broke all over again when she realized she was losing the baby.

Sigh. So many of her decisions back then had been a result of what had happened between her and Dex.

Looking back, she could see that Gabe might have been a rebound boyfriend. She'd been so blinded by grief from everything that she might have jumped into that relationship before she'd gotten over any of it.

And she'd paid a steep price for that mistake.

Well, she wasn't going to pay the price for a second one. She needed to be very, very careful how she behaved around him. Heaven only knew she was still just as taken by his looks as she'd been back then. And by even the most casual of touches. So she needed to tread with care, or she was going to wind up being hurt all over again.

And this time that hurt might be harder to get over than it had been last time.

Ha! Last time? She wasn't sure she'd ever completely gotten over it.

But if not, she needed to do whatever it took to keep those embers from bursting back to life.

She was going to douse them with water

every time a spark appeared. Again and again, for as long as it took for them to believe the truth: that she and Dex had been over—for a very long time.

CHAPTER FOUR

THE HOSPITAL APPROVED the funding for the women's crisis center project a week later. A week in which Dex had had the chance to examine the whys of his suggestion with eyes that were a bit clearer than they'd been. Now he was wondering what the hell he'd gotten himself into. Especially since the hospital administrator had suggested he and Maura head it up and hold a Christmas party for the moms and kids in the hospital's name, buying presents and funding a big meal.

What if the center was already planning a party? he'd asked. The response had been: Well, then they'd add to it—make it something extra special.

He doubted the crisis center had the funds to host a big celebration. But the hospital had some donors with deep pockets, and they were all for it. Especially since this would be great publicity. The center, which had seen such tragedy, would have its spirits revived by the hospital that had saved one of their own.

As much as he hated his cynicism, he could see the hospital's point, except now he was having to help the hospital use that tragedy for its own benefit. What was worse was that the hospital had said it would be great if fate gave them snow on that day.

Even better? Not for him.

He'd yet to break the news to Maura yet. She'd probably be thrilled by the prospect.

Dex and his big mouth.

On a good note, the gunshot victim was slowly recovering. Her EEG readings were promising, as was her ability to speak and reason, although she was still slurring her words a bit.

He folded the papers with the funding amounts and shoved it in his pocket. The patient had been moved from ICU to a regular room this morning, and he wanted to check on her and see how she was doing.

Giving a sigh, he made his way down the hallway to room 205, giving a quick knock on the door before pushing through it. "Hi, Sylvia, how are you feeling today?"

Just then, he noticed the chair pulled up beside the bed and the person in it, holding a squirming child. "Maura?"

She glanced at him with a smile that made his mouth go dry as she shifted the child back onto her lap. "You can't sit on Mommy right now. She has some boo-boos that need to heal."

Ah, this was Sylvia's child. Just then the dark-haired boy broke free and darted toward the bed. Dex intercepted him, scooping him into his arms. "Where do you think you're going, young man?"

The boy looked up at him with a surprised expression, and Dex willed the child not to cry. He didn't. Instead, he giggled. "Do again."

He blinked unsure of what the boy meant, then he got it. He lifted the child, swooping him into the air and pivoting on his heel. Just in time to catch the openmouthed shock on Maura's face. He propped the child on his hip and pretended it was no big deal, even though it was. He wasn't sure what had prompted him to play "airplane" with a complete stranger's child. Especially since he'd never felt particularly comfortable around children.

"What's his name?"

Sylvia spoke slowly, carefully enunciating each syllable separately. "Wes…ton."

He pretended not to notice the difficulty she had in saying the name. "Weston, huh? How old are you, kiddo?"

The child held up three fingers one at a time. "I free."

"Free" for three?

"Well, a big boy like you can sit in a chair for a minute. How about if I give you some paper to color on?"

"Color!"

He felt his pockets and drew out the papers from the administrator, turning them over and thinking, *To hell with it.* If the hospital wanted a party for kids, this was part and parcel of that.

He found a pen and laid it on top of the pages.

Weston started scribbling on the back of the page, while Dex took Sylvia's vitals and discreetly checked the bandages covering her wounds. Everything looked good. "Your pain levels are okay?"

Part of the slurred speech could be the result of the heavy painkillers they were using to help alleviate her discomfort. Fortunately, the woman didn't have a history of drug use, which would have made the situation more complicated. According to the rest of the staff, she hadn't asked about her ex. Maybe the things that had happened that day were still blurry. Or maybe she'd blocked them out. He couldn't blame her if that was the case.

He glanced at Maura, wondering what they'd talked about before he got there, and how she'd managed to bring Weston to visit. She'd obviously been over to the center, which made a little pinpoint of discomfort stir in his gut.

She's a grown woman, Dex. She doesn't need your permission or anyone else's.

Besides, that's how he'd gotten into this mess of a Christmas party.

So he asked a completely unrelated question. "How is Weston getting home?"

She looked at him. "I'm taking him back in a few minutes. Sylvia had asked if he was allowed to see her. Her doctors said yes." She tossed a smile at Sylvia. "And I thought it would be good for her."

Hmm... Dex was one of Sylvia's doctors, and Maura hadn't asked him. Maybe she wanted as little to do with him as possible, which didn't bode well for them working together.

"I wanted...to make...sure...he was... okay." Sylvia's eyes filled with tears that spilled over.

So she did remember what had happened. If she'd been carrying the child out of the center the day she'd been shot... Hell, he didn't even want to think about the fact that they might have had two patients. Or maybe her ex had planned it to be a murder/suicide all along.

"He's just fine, as you can see. The staff is taking great care of him."

He wondered if someone from the center was staying with the boy in their assigned room. Maura had mentioned that a couple of staff members were approved foster parents. If so, he was glad the child's world wasn't going to be upended more than it already was.

Another good thing was that Weston was too young to really remember much about his father. Hopefully, the abuse hadn't extended to the child.

"I'm off duty, so I'll go with you to take him back to the women's center. I have something I want to talk to you about, anyway."

Her glance shot his way, the dismay in her eyes unmistakable. "You do?"

"It's nothing major."

Ha! It was pretty major, actually. But he wasn't going to say anything in front of Sylvia, especially since he wasn't sure how Maura was going to take the news. What had started off as a simple class in first aid had morphed into a full-blown hospital-funded publicity event. Hell, he wasn't sure how he felt about it, himself. It seemed like recently he'd been sticking his nose where it didn't belong and getting it singed in the process.

Well, it stopped after this. They had three weeks before Christmas, and then it would be over. As would everything else they did together. Except for maybe teaching a class or two together.

As much as it pained him to admit it,

though, in all the dismay over this, there was an element of anticipation. Hadn't he been thinking about how he could give back? Maybe this was the beginning of that. He still planned to apply to Doctors Without Borders, but instead of dwelling on how much he hated winter, he could keep himself busy and do some good in the process.

Sylvia had zoned out and looked like she was falling asleep. He glanced at Maura to see that she'd noticed as well. She stood and laid a hand on the other woman's arm. "Hey, we're going to take Weston back. You need your rest."

"When can I go...?" Sylvia tried to lift herself off the pillow, but failed and fell back, drawing a deep breath. "When can I go back and be with him?"

It would be weeks before she was well enough to get out of the hospital. She had no idea how close she'd come to dying. If they hadn't been able to clamp off that artery when they had...

Her organs were going to need time to recover from the shock. And so was her mind.

"You don't worry about that," Maura said.

"You concentrate on getting stronger. You can only do that if you rest."

"Okay." She reached out a hand to Weston.

Dex picked the boy up and carried him over to his mother. She held his hand in hers. "I love you, Wes."

The boy wriggled a little, trying to get to her, but Dex held him tight. The last thing she needed was for him to bounce on her wounds. "We'll bring him back soon."

When he turned around, Maura had the paper Weston had colored on and was looking at the other side of it, her brows puckered. "What's this?"

"Uh...yeah, that's what I wanted to talk to you about. Ready?"

She stared at him for a second before taking Weston's hand and waving it at his mom. "Say bye, honey."

"Bye, baby. See you soon."

Then they were out of the door and heading down the hallway. "I need to get my coat and hat," she said. "And I'm serious. What is this?"

As she got her winter gear on, he explained as best he could.

"Remember me asking you to hold off on giving the center an answer, that the hospital might want to contribute to the educational effort? Well, they do. Only they want to do more. They feel like having a Christmas party will help build goodwill between the hospital and the community, especially after what happened to Sylvia."

"What happened wasn't the hospital's fault." She tucked a strand of hair behind her ear so that it stayed toward the back of her knit cap.

"I know that and you know that, but they think if they use the whole turn-a-tragedy-into-something-good plan, it might turn the hospital into a kind of hero." He shrugged. "And the center might get something good out of it, as well. Like an increase in donations or volunteers. Or maybe job offers for the residents who need them."

She still looked dubious, but at least she didn't look angry. And *dubious* suited her. Her eyebrows were puckered in a way that drew attention to those dark eyes. Eyes that shimmered with compassion and a little something else.

"So you're going to do what? Play jolly old Saint Nick, while passing out presents?"

"Me? No. I'll leave that for someone who believes a little more in the season."

They went outside, and he started toward his car only to have her stop him. "I'll drive. I already have Weston's car seat buckled in." She grinned. "It took quite a while to figure it out. I even had to ask Mr. Google for his help. I'd rather not have to go through that all over again—unless you know how to install it in your car?"

Maura's smile had never failed to take his breath away back when they were dating. It still did. Those pink curving lips pointed at the delicate bones in her cheeks, hollowing them out underneath. In fact, she was a little more slender than she'd been back then. Maybe it was the stress of her divorce, since it had only been a year ago. He was surprised she'd never had children with her husband. Maybe her miscarriage had done something that made that impossible.

Something jabbed his midsection at that thought.

Before most of his family had died in that

accident, he'd pictured Maura and himself married with three or four children. Of course that had all changed in an instant and left him wanting no ties at all. Not to a wife. Not to children.

Even his relationship with his mom had been strained over the years, despite him staying in Montana in case she needed something, especially as she hadn't remarried. She'd gathered her friends around her as she'd grieved. Those friends had helped her more than Dex had, which just added to his guilt. He knew he'd been distant and apathetic, but he hadn't been sure how to be anything else back then. That apathy had become a habit that he'd had a hard time tossing aside. And he wasn't sure he wanted to, at this point.

Seeing Sylvia almost lose her own life had just brought home all the reasons for his apathy. If she'd died, her son's life would have changed forever.

Just like Dex's had.

No, it was better when he only had himself to worry about.

Why had he been so insistent on helping Maura hold classes at the women's center?

Because he'd been uneasy with her being there alone—at night. Although he couldn't afford to have her in his life, there was still a part of him that needed to know she shared the same world he did. That he only needed to walk through her department to catch sight of her. Or pick up a phone to hear her voice.

Not that he would call her—it was just the assurance that she was still here. That her heart was still beating in her chest. That she could sigh and smile...and *live*.

It was the whole reason he hadn't gone after her the day of their breakup.

"Okay, your car it is."

They reached it, a little red compact that fit her to a tee. "You sure like the color red, don't you?"

She had a red coat. A red hat. And now a red car.

"I never really thought about it." She glanced down at her coat. "I guess maybe I do."

She opened the door and pulled his seat forward to be able to get Weston into his car seat in back. It was a little more complicated with a two-door, but they managed. When

Dex went to slide into the passenger seat, his knees pressed into the dashboard.

She laughed. "Sorry. I don't normally have anyone riding in that seat. I pulled it way forward because of Weston. The handle is on the side."

Tugging on the lever, he pushed the seat back a couple of inches, careful not to crush Weston's legs. He was beginning to think maybe they should have wrestled the boy's car seat into his BMW after all.

"I bet you get great gas mileage in this thing."

One thing he was doing his best not to think about was how this vehicle might crumple if she ever hit anything. Or if anything hit her.

Something in his throat tightened.

"As a matter of fact I do." She tossed her hair, buckling her seat belt. "I'm all about efficiency in every area of my life."

Was that why she'd dumped him all those years ago—because he messed with her sense of efficiency? No, she'd dumped him because he wouldn't—couldn't—give her what she wanted: the security of knowing she was The

One for him. She'd done the right thing when he'd hemmed and hawed over an answer.

They dropped Weston off at the center, and Maura gave the director an update in quick, concise phrases. And although her words matched her whole "efficiency" line, there was an undertone of compassion that didn't seem to fit into her self-described box. He liked the juxtaposition of soft crocheted blankets and her cramped fuel-efficient car. It was a complicated mixture. As was everything about Maura.

It was one of the things that had attracted him to her in the first place. And he was finding it still attracted him. She'd been all about academics in high school, and yet she had this laugh that came straight from her belly and poured over him. A laugh that could still make his body tighten, even today.

She'd challenged him to be a better student back then. She'd taught him some study techniques after class. And seeing the dark hair slide over her cheek as she explained shortcuts that worked for her had made his teenage hormones ramp into overdrive. No other girl had done that for him.

Then or now.

Their first kiss had happened standing beside their creek as the snow drifted down around them. Her lips had been warm and soft, her breath sliding in gentle gusts over his chilled skin. He'd had a hard time pulling away and walking her home.

Hell. The best and worst moments of his life had happened in the snow.

They got back into the car a few minutes later. "So tell me about those papers Weston was drawing on. I thought you were asking for help with classes like the first aid one."

"I was. The hospital wanted that and more, like I told you earlier."

"Well, I could use a coffee…or a drink. So if you can stand being confined to my car for a few more minutes, we can go back to my place and you can tell me exactly what the hospital wants. And I'll tell you whether or not I'm willing to go along with it. If not, I'm still going to do a first-aid class they asked me to do. New Billings Memorial can fire me, if they want, but they can't stop me."

Great, this wasn't quite how he'd envisioned this going, although he hadn't been all that thrilled, either, when he'd walked out of the administrator's office with the paperwork. Paperwork they would both need to sign if this was to happen. And really, without Maura—who the center already knew and trusted—he couldn't see the director letting a bunch of strangers in there, Christmas party or no Christmas party. He couldn't blame them. Especially not after what had happened to Sylvia.

"Coffee sounds good." Actually, a stiff drink sounded better, but he'd take what he could get at this point.

Fifteen minutes later, while Maura made coffee, Dex wandered around her living room. The space was sparse, almost cold, with furniture that looked like it came straight out of one of those nail-it-together-yourself stores. Mostly white and beige, there were no pops of color. No framed artwork on the walls. No books littering the end tables. It all seemed strange to him. Despite being a straight-A student, the Maura he'd once dated had been warm and welcoming…messy and carefree. This new Maura had a place for everything. Maybe she'd always been this way, and he just hadn't recognized it back then. She'd certainly needed to find exactly where she fit in his life. And when he wouldn't help her do that...

Back to the same old tired arguments he'd had after his dad and siblings died. Coming here was probably a mistake on his part. He'd been fine working at the same hospital when their paths rarely crossed. But all of a sudden here they were—having coffee and getting ready to discuss working together on a much deeper level than they did at the hospital. The fact that this was a project neither of them really wanted didn't help matters.

She came into the room carrying a white tray and an equally white coffee carafe. Each new thing made him a little more uneasy. Was this colorless space the place she'd lived with her ex-husband? Had her marriage fit into this same boring mold?

Because there'd been nothing boring about what Dex had shared with her. That fact made him take stock, as well. Surely their breakup had not caused that big a change.

Maybe her husband hadn't been a fan of

color. Maybe she'd adapted to make him happy.

Except her crocheted blankets were filled with all kinds of different hues. He hadn't seen a beige or white one in the bunch. And then there was that red coat and hat. Which was the real Maura? The one she gathered around her in the privacy of her home? Or the one he'd once known?

Setting the tray down, she poured their brew into mugs and set one in front of him. "I wasn't sure what you took in yours, so there's sugar and cream."

"Black is fine." He accepted the proffered mug and took a sip. "Thanks."

"So, you want me to ask the director if the hospital can throw a Christmas party?"

He looked at her over the cup and paused as he thought through his answer. "I think it has to come from you. The center trusts you. So do the clients and the administration. Look at Celia and Sylvia. And even Weston."

"So if I say no, the hospital won't ask about throwing one?"

"I don't think they will. And I'm pretty

sure the center isn't going to let a bunch of strangers go in there and take over."

She balanced her mug on her knee. "And what do you think of all this? Do you think we should give the hospital what they want?"

"I think we should do what's best for the residents of that center and their children."

"That's what I was afraid you were going to say." She sighed and closed her eyes for a minute. When she opened them, they were warm and met his with a sincerity that took his breath away. A sincerity that made him want to cup her face in his hands and get lost in those dark brown irises. "I think we should have this party, Dex. Not because of the hospital, but because those women and kids deserve it."

Before he could stop himself, he said. "I think they do, too."

"I wish I could take their pain away and make every one of them feel safe and loved."

That was the problem. Sometimes you couldn't, no matter how much you wanted to. "No one can do that for anyone. The best you can hope for is to show you care and point toward resources that can help them cope."

Except how many times had people tried to send him to grief counseling groups only to have him refuse to go, to shrug things off as if they were no big deal?

"I know. I just want to do more."

"Making those blankets is more. Taking Weston to the hospital to visit his mom is more." He smiled. "Having this Christmas party is more."

She tilted her head and regarded him. "I never thought about it like that."

"You've been a good influence on me, believe it or not. And not just when I was a dumb kid. Taking those blankets to the center that day made me take stock of my own life and how little I give back to the world around me." It was true. His thoughts about Doctors Without Borders had crystallized over the past week. He'd even contacted the organization yesterday about getting paperwork to start the process.

After taking one last sip of his coffee, he set down the cup. "So we'll have the party, and it will make me feel like I've given back, if only in a minuscule way."

"It won't be minuscule to those women." She paused for a few seconds. "Or to me."

Or to me.

The words made him look at her. Really look.

Her eyes shone with a warmth and hope that made the breath hiss from his lungs.

Damn, she was the most gorgeous thing he'd ever seen. In this pale room, she was the only thing that was vibrant. Colorful.

Alive.

Her dark hair shimmered against the cream-colored sofa, and her lips were soft and pink and would be so very...

Warm. Just like at the creek all those years ago.

A tingling started in regions best left alone. "I should go."

"Okay." She gave a visible swallow. "If you think you should."

The way she said that...

Hell, he didn't only *think* he should, he *knew* he should. "Unless you think we should do a little more planning."

Maura gripped her coffee mug. "Planning. Yes."

Planning was the last thing on his mind.

A thousand memories from long ago sailed through his head, getting caught up in the stormy recesses. Some sweet, some incredibly hot and sexy. They kept spinning through his mind until he could no longer separate one from the other.

Or yesterday from today. It was all twined together in a cacophony that was impossible to mute. And he didn't want to. Maura was part of the fabric that made him who he was today, despite them being no longer together.

He resisted the urge to reach for her, even as he struggled with the need to tell her the truth—that he was headed down a dangerous path, one he couldn't seem to veer away from. Honesty won.

"Maura, I don't want to plan the party."

"You don't?"

"Hell, I know we should. I know that's what I came here for. But I can't stop thinking about…you."

Her cup went onto the tray, and she inched closer, her fingers going to his cheek and trailing down the side of his face. Her eyes closed as if trying to capture the feel and post it to memory, just as he had. "That's funny, because I was just thinking about you."

He leaned forward and pressed his forehead to hers. "You were supposed to make me listen to reason."

She laughed. "Right now, I can't think of a single reasonable thing to say."

His hand slid beneath her hair and cupped her nape, and he leaned back to look at her. And yep, the feeling was still there, getting stronger by the second. So he took one long, deep breath before plunging beneath the water and putting his lips to hers.

CHAPTER FIVE

HOW HAD THIS HAPPENED?

One minute they were talking about helping the women and kids at the crisis center
and the next he was kissing her.

And not just any kiss. It was hot and deep
and rivaled anything they'd done in the past.
And some of those meetings of the lips had
made her go weak in the knees at the time.

She was finding out they still did.

To be honest, she'd wanted this since he'd
stopped and helped her the day she'd had the
flat tire, and when he'd gone with her to de-
liver the afghans. She'd seen something in
his face that said he understood what she was
trying to do for those women. The knowledge
had made a familiar yearning come roaring
back down the road, heading straight toward
her. She'd avoided him for so long, and maybe

it had been the wrong thing to do. Maybe this kiss was part of that elusive thing called closure.

His lips moved, dragging her attention back to the luscious things he was doing to her mouth. To hell with closure. She could worry about that later. Right now, all she wanted was…this.

Her tongue edged forward, nudging at the entrance to his mouth, and he opened and captured it with a suddenness that took her breath away, using gentle suction to pull her inside.

He was hot, with an intensity that was chipping away at the edges of her self-control, making her want a whole lot more than what he was giving. She twisted sideways in an attempt to get closer, her hands sliding over his shoulders and gripping tight.

Don't stop, Dex. Please, God, don't stop.

He didn't.

Half-dragging her over his lap, he set her so she was straddling him, and the quick change from a kiss that was anything but chaste to full-on contact sent her mind spinning. "God, Dex…"

His fingers tunneled into her hair as he held her against his lips. "I love hearing you say that."

One hand went to her butt, hauling her against him until she felt exactly what she was doing to him…what he was doing to her. She wanted him. Wanted to rip off his clothes and feel him thrust home, like he'd done so many times before.

This position had always been one of their favorites. How could she have forgotten?

In his car. By the creek. In his bed. He loved her on top of him, loved gripping her hips and guiding her as she rode him to completion. Then the aftermath of those times had been…

So sweet. So…them. Their own secret world where nothing else intruded.

She needed that again. Wanted it.

In a split second, she made a decision. She nipped his lip before reaching down and grabbing the hem of his polo shirt, hauling it up and over his head. There was no hesitation as he helped her. He leaned back and watched her unbutton her own shirt, taking it from her and tossing it to the side.

Warm hands skated up her belly, making her muscles ripple as they went before cupping her breasts, his thumbs finding her nipples under the fabric of her bra with laser accuracy.

It was just like before. Just like she knew it would be.

"Are you sure, Maura? Tell me now, if not."

"Ahh…yes. I'm sure." She let her body answer any other questions as she arched into him, relishing it when one hand reached behind her back for the clasp and undid it. It soon joined the other pieces of discarded clothing. Then, with one palm against her bare back, he drew her forward until his mouth found her, suckling and nipping at her sensitized flesh. A flame of need shot straight to her center, and she pressed tighter against him in an effort to keep it at bay. It didn't work. And the pressure inside of her was beginning to build in a familiar way.

No, not yet. Please not yet.

"Hell, Maura. I need to get those pants off you. But I don't. Want. You. To. Move." Each word was punctuated with another pull on her nipple.

Leaning her face against his neck, she gave a pained laugh. "I don't want to move either, especially when you're doing that. But here goes."

She hauled herself off his lap and, with hands that shook, she shed her slacks, hesitating at her underwear before shoving them down her legs. He was busy doing the same, retrieving something from the pocket of his khakis as he went.

A condom.

The shot of regret came out of nowhere, piercing her heart and causing a burst of pain before she beat it back. It wouldn't happen again. It couldn't. He was making sure of it.

The fact that she hadn't given a thought to protection, even after what had happened in the past, was a testament to how much this man disrupted her thought processes.

But right now, she needed him. Needed to forget the horror that had happened at the women's center with Sylvia. Tragedy could strike anyone anywhere. So why not live in this moment and just let herself feel. Experience. *Live.*

When Dex held his arms out to her, she

went willingly—gladly—settling back on his lap and closing her eyes at the utter ecstasy that came with feeling him again, skin to skin. "I'd almost forgotten…"

She couldn't finish the sentence, but it was true. She'd forgotten so much, and yet the second she was with him, it all came rushing back.

"I know."

Those two words were profound, and she knew he wasn't saying that he knew she'd forgotten, but that he too had just experienced the very same thing.

Her first time with Gabe hadn't been like this…an overwhelming connection of one person to another. She'd assumed it was because there were no "firsts" like that "first" first. She was wrong. Being with Dex, after so many years had passed, made it happen all over again. And she remembered every second of her first time with him.

They stayed like that for a minute or two before Dex's lips gently touched hers, and soon it was washing over her again. The need. The longing. The craving for a release that only he could give.

She wanted him inside. Now.

Taking the packet from beside his thigh, she ripped it open and slid back far enough to expose him, to slide the condom down him with a slow, smooth stroke that had him groaning.

Her lips curved. Dex had always been a vocal lover, holding nothing back. And she'd loved it. Had missed it.

Not letting go of him, she raised her hips and lowered herself onto him. His flesh was hot, stretching her in ways that made her weak. Her breath exited with a hum that changed to something that defied words. Or logic. Something that wiped away thoughts of the women's center, the hospital…and even their own past.

The only thing that mattered was what was right in front of her.

His fingers wrapped around her hips as she found a rhythm and an angle that was so very perfect. Her body remembered. Sought out what she knew was there.

Each time she lowered onto him, it sent shock waves through her. Those waves grew with each thrust, the intensity making her cup his face and kiss him.

Tongues tangled. Teeth found hidden nerve endings. Need ratcheted everything to a new level of ecstasy.

He urged her to move faster, take him deeper, which had her matching him thrust for thrust until her whole world shifted with a suddenness that took her breath away. Something ignited deep inside of her, the spark becoming a flame that devoured everything in its path.

It grew hotter. Brighter. Then exploded in a fury of want and need that swallowed her whole. He joined her almost immediately, muttering words against her skin that her brain couldn't process—didn't want to process.

Then it was over. She lowered herself onto him one last time as the final tiny spasms worked their way out of her system. Breathing heavily, she closed her eyes and leaned against him, waiting for her senses to return. For the sweet aftermath to take over, like it had in the past.

And all too soon, it did. But it wasn't the

same, wasn't as sweet as she remembered. Because *they* weren't the same. They were no longer that carefree couple who could love each other without reserve.

They were…strangers.

She swallowed as cold reality of that word washed over her. She'd just had sex with a man she had once loved. A man who hadn't been able to commit to her—who hadn't *wanted* to commit to her. Who'd left her brokenhearted, carrying a child she hadn't been able to tell him about. All because she didn't want him staying for any reasons other than love.

Why? Why now?

Maybe it was muscle memory. Maybe an old neural pathway she hadn't been able to entirely obliterate.

Whatever it was, it wasn't happening again.

Climbing off his lap as gracefully as she could manage, she began gathering her clothes, yanking them on with a fury that was aimed squarely at herself.

A hand wrapped around her wrist, stopping her just as she'd shrugged into her bra. "Hey. Stop for a minute. Are you okay?"

"Just peachy, Dex. Can't you tell?" Realizing the words were said with a bitterness she hadn't been able to disguise, she glanced over at him. "This was a mistake, and you know it."

"Yes. And I'm sorry. I don't know what got into me."

It was unfair of her to let him take the brunt of her anger. "Hell, it wasn't you. It was me, you…both of us."

She searched around for something more to say. "It just can't happen again. I've had two failed relationships now, and this—" she motioned at the rest of their clothes "—is something I just can't handle right now."

"I understand." He turned her toward him, tipping up her chin. "And it won't happen again. I promise."

The solemnity of those words made tears prick behind her eyes. What had she been hoping for? That he would say he'd been wrong all those years ago? That he'd never stopped loving her?

She had no idea. But as great as the sex was, there was an ache gnawing at her insides that hadn't been touched by what they'd just done.

The tears grew when his hands went behind her and gently redid the clasp on her bra. "What can I do to make this right?"

She shrugged, not meeting his eyes. "There's nothing to make right, because what just happened means nothing. Changes nothing. And I don't want it to. I just want us to go back to whatever professional relationship we had before this, and to pretend it never happened."

"Pretend." He said the word in a musing tone as if trying to figure out what it meant.

And she was right. It would all be pretend. Because as much as she might wish otherwise, nothing was going to change what had happened in this room. Every time she sat on her sofa, she would picture him under her, moving inside of her. Every. Damn. Time.

She didn't know what she was going to do about that, but she'd better figure it out. And soon. Because the last thing Maura needed was to let a man who'd once wrought devastation in her heart slide past her defenses all over again.

She was going to do exactly what she'd said she was going to do: pretend. And hope to hell that if she did it often enough and for long enough, her heart would eventually believe it to be true.

Dex leaned over his sink and gave himself a long, hard look. He'd been selfish and careless...and wrong.

Two days later he was still beating himself up over what had happened at Maura's place. He never should have gone to her house to discuss the Christmas party. They should have done it at the hospital. In a coffee shop. At the zoo. Anyplace but somewhere private. Because he knew himself well enough to know that as much as he might deny it, he'd never gotten over Maura. Yesterday had proved that beyond a shadow of a doubt.

He also knew that he wasn't in a place for that to change anything. He was still the same miserable, empty guy he had been the day Maura had broken things off.

He should tell the administration that he couldn't do the Christmas party, to find someone else. But wouldn't that be just as selfish as sleeping with her? He was an adult. He could work with her. She'd said as much, that she wanted to go back to their professional relationship and forget what had happened.

No, she hadn't used the word *forget*. She'd used the word *pretend*. There was a huge difference between the two. He just wasn't sure why that difference mattered so much.

Maybe because he didn't want to forget. Oh, he could pretend along with the best of them. But forget? That was in a different category entirely.

It would have been so much easier if Maura was still married.

Really? Somehow, he doubted that. Oh, he might have managed not to have sex with her two days ago, but then again, he probably wouldn't have wound up in her house, like an idiot.

He knew absolutely that Maura wouldn't have made that offer if she wasn't damned sure it was safe. He'd known better, and he'd gone anyway. But there'd been that knife edge of adrenaline urging him on, telling him he could resist his own urges. Like those worst-ideas-in-the-world videos, it had backfired spectacularly.

And he'd ended up hurting her. Again.

She'd never said it outright, but it had been there in her eyes. In the frantic way she'd grabbed her clothes. In the way she'd said, *I can't do this again.*

Everything pointed to the fact that he was the only one who'd exited that room un-scathed.

Really? He wouldn't quite characterize it that way.

And today they had a meeting with Colleen Winters from the Nadia Ram Crisis Center for Mothers about what the hospital was offering to do in a little under three weeks.

Worse, Sylvia was due to be discharged today, and when he'd spoken to the director on the phone, he'd offered to drive her back, since the center was short staffed today.

So were his brain cells, which were barely capable of putting two and two together without coming up with some outrageous number combinations.

He turned away from the mirror and finished getting dressed. He hadn't talked to

Maura except in passing since that day at her place. But the hospital's administrative director said he'd spoken with her, and she'd freed up her schedule to go with him to talk to the center's director. But she hadn't called or texted to let him know she was on board. Maybe she was leaving it up to him.

Which meant he needed to do so—and quick, since the meeting with Colleen was today.

Wrapping a towel around his waist, he retrieved his cell phone and punched her number into it.

He could do this.

He waited through two, three, four rings and then her voice mail picked up. Great. She didn't want to talk to him. "Just checking in about our meeting today…"

Even as he was trying to lay out his explanation, his phone started buzzing in his hand. She was calling him back. He took a quick breath before clicking to accept the call, then put the phone to his ear. "Sorry, I was just leaving you a message."

"It's okay, I was getting ready for work."

He glanced down at himself. Was she in the

same state of undress that he was? An image shot through his brain before he could stop it. He blinked it away. It didn't matter, and he certainly wasn't going to ask.

"I was checking on our meeting at the center?"

"Oh. Yes."

Was she going to tell him that she wasn't going to participate, not even to teach the first aid class? A pool of acid formed in his stomach and churned up his esophagus. If that was the case, he was going to withdraw so that she could carry on without him. It wasn't right for her to have to sit out on something that meant so much to her.

"You're still interested in being a part, aren't you?"

"Of course, why wouldn't I be?" Her words were stilted—overly formal.

We can just pretend it never happened.

She was taking those words and making them true. Well, two could play that game. "No reason. I thought we could ride over together, since we're supposed to take Sylvia back to the center."

"I can drive, if you'd like."

The image of her tiny vehicle with its cramped quarters came back to mind. He'd be close to her. Way too close. "How about if we take my car this time, since we took yours the last time?"

A slight pause ensued. "Of course. When would you like to meet?"

He hated how impersonal those words were, even though he knew he was the cause of it. "How about if I check to see what time Sylvia is going to be discharged this afternoon and let you know?"

"Three o'clock."

"Sorry?"

"I've already checked with the hospital and they said her discharge time is three."

So had she decided to go over without him? Maybe his call had tossed a monkey wrench into her plans. "Would you rather I not be there today, Maura?"

A noise he thought might be a sigh came through the line. "I'm sorry, Dex. This is just a little awkward. But it'll be okay. I think Sylvia would like you to be a part, since you had a hand in saving her life."

"Not really."

"Um… You held her artery in your hand. Literally. So please don't say that to her. She sees you as an example of what a man should be like. Don't take that away from her. She's grateful—let her show it in whatever way she can."

It was ironic that a victim of domestic violence would think he was a good example of what a man should be. Especially since he was struggling with his image of himself this morning.

"Okay, we'll meet in Sylvia's room at around three, then? Or should we meet a half hour before that to plan our approach for the center?" Maura said.

"That works for me, since you know them a lot better than I do. How about in the waiting room?" A part of him was relieved that she was still okay with working with him on the Christmas party, even though it probably wasn't very smart of him. Well, he could just suck it up and deal with it. It was not quite three weeks of his life. Surely he could manage that.

Hadn't he already given himself this same lecture once before? It hadn't done him much good last time. What made him think this time would be any different?

Because he now knew what could happen if he was caught off guard, and he intended to make sure that never happened again.

From now on, he would be on high alert and spot trouble before it headed his way.

Easier said than done since, to his psyche, Maura was the epitome of trouble.

"Okay, see you there."

What he did over the next couple of weeks would say a lot about whether or not Sylvia's view of him was true. Or whether she was completely off base. If that was the case, the best thing he could do was pretend to be something he couldn't be in real life.

Two thirty came a lot quicker than he'd thought it would. And by the time he got to the waiting room, Maura was already there.

"Hey."

"Hi."

His teeth ground against themselves. Not because of the awkwardness, but because his mind was replaying every second they'd spent on that sofa. And that was not acceptable.

Lowering himself onto the seat across

from hers, he unfolded the paperwork from the hospital, Weston's scribbling staring up at him. Okay. This was why he was here. To talk about Weston, Sylvia and the women at that shelter.

"So…thoughts? Do you think they'll go for letting the hospital take part in the Christmas celebration?"

"I think so. I made a quick call to Colleen and asked if she'd be open to funding or help to give the residents a good Christmas. She seemed relieved. Said that she had actually been worried about it this year. It seems with the fires in California this year, most people's thoughts are on that—and rightly so— but funding sources have dried up."

He hadn't thought about that, although the reports had been all over the news. "Maybe the hospital's offer came at a good time, then."

"I think maybe it did. I think we should make this something fun. Not formal like a gala or prom with fancy dresses."

He smiled. "No turquoise dresses?"

"Don't remind me." She laughed. "That dress was a disaster."

So she did remember. "At the time I was

pretty happy that it was a bit long. You kept tripping and I had to keep catching you."

"I didn't make a very good impression."

Yes, she had. She'd made the best one possible. Only going down these old pathways probably wasn't going to help either one of them. "It actually helped settle my nerves."

"Nerves? You were always so sure of yourself."

Not when it came to her. Not then, and certainly not now.

"Believe me, I get nervous. I'm a little on edge about this meeting, actually."

"Don't be. Colleen is great."

The subject turned back to the matter at hand, and if anything, Maura's tone held a hint of excitement as she gave some insight into the center and the director who headed it up. "If she agrees, then I can guarantee the residents will, as well. They all love and respect her."

"So you said you wanted the party to be fun. Any ideas on that?"

"I do, but let's feel her out before jumping into that part. Especially since it might be a little outside of the normal Christmas box."

He thought about her monochromatic living room and how her current life seemed to be about keeping everything inside of the box. "Christmas boxes are meant to be opened, though, aren't they?"

"You could be on to something there."

He was definitely curious now. What did outside of the box look like to this new Maura? "Sure you can't give me a hint?"

Her grin made her nose crinkle in an old, familiar way. He forced himself to glance away before it affected him in ways that were just as familiar.

"Let's wait and see how the meeting goes before we start doing any real planning."

Start doing any real planning. So she was actually thinking of this as being a team effort. One that included him.

The little sliver of anticipation he'd had when he'd reached the waiting room ramped up to something a whole lot more. Something that he should be running away from as fast as his legs could carry him. Instead, he leaned forward. "I can't wait to hear all about it."

It had been right to use Dex's car. It had a lot more space for Sylvia, who at a little over a week out of surgery was still sore and weak.

But she was anxious to get back to her son. They helped her out of the wheelchair and into the back seat of the car. Thankfully, the reporters had cleared out the day after the shooting had happened. For that Maura was grateful. The last thing Sylvia needed was to face them or have someone stick a microphone in her face.

"Are you okay?" she asked, knowing immediately that it was a stupid question. Sylvia had not only left an abusive husband, that same husband she'd once loved had then shot and almost killed her before turning the gun on himself. Nothing would erase that.

Maura's problems with Dex seemed ludicrous compared to what the other woman had gone through. And during their impromptu meeting at the hospital, she realized she'd probably been too hard on both of them after they'd had sex. But the aftermath of being intimate with him again had hit her with such force that panic had overwhelmed her and she'd taken that panic out on him.

Unfairly.

"I'm okay. I'll be glad to see Weston."

"You need to make sure you don't do too

much too soon. You're still healing. He can't jump on you."

"I know. The lady from the center who's been taking care of him will still help with him. It's the only way the hospital would let me go without sending me to a skilled nursing facility."

It might not have been a bad idea for her to have gone to one for a few weeks, but Sylvia had been adamant about going back to the shelter. And who could blame her? Christmas was rapidly approaching, and she had a young child to think about.

Maura paused before closing the door. "What's Weston's favorite animal?"

Sylvia chuckled before giving a quick grimace of pain. "A giraffe of all things. His room back..." Her voice fell to a whisper. "His room in the house we lived at was decorated with them. He had to leave his favorite one behind when we left."

Maura's heart ached for both of them. "Will you go back there?"

"No. The house was already in foreclosure. Things got a whole lot worse once Clyde got the papers in the mail."

Time to turn Sylvia's thoughts toward the future. "Well, that's all behind you now. You can finally finish that nursing degree you started."

"Yes, that's what I want to do. I want to make a better life for my boy."

"For yourself, as well. And you already are." Maura shut the door and moved around to the front seat. She'd tried to get Sylvia to sit there, but she'd refused, and Dex thought maybe sitting sideways would help take some of the pressure off her healing wounds. He'd been right.

At least about that.

She slid into the passenger seat and glanced over at Dex, who nodded at her. "I bet the hospital has some educational grant programs we can look into."

The words were meant for Sylvia, but they warmed Maura's heart. He was a good man. So many times she'd looked at the past and wished things had been different. That his dad and siblings were still alive and life had gone the way they'd planned. She had no idea what it was like losing a twin, let alone losing that twin along with a younger sister and a father, but Dex had changed after that.

Would their baby have looked like him?

She'd argued with herself repeatedly that losing the child had been for the best. But she never quite believed it. She was pretty sure Sylvia was glad she'd had Weston, despite the circumstances. That he was the one bright spot in a tragic situation. Maura's baby could have been that bright spot. The one good thing that would have come out of their failed relationship.

Except Dex would have known. And what had been a sad moment in her life would have become a sad—and complicated—moment that would have linked the two of them for the rest of her life.

No, better that it ended the way it did.

And sex with him?

Just a speed bump in the road that made up her life. A warning not to let herself race ahead when she needed to slow down and take stock of where she was.

Unfortunately, she'd hit that bump at full speed and had become airborne for several exhilarating minutes. Still, what goes up must come down, and the shock of that landing was still reverberating through her She was pretty sure she might have left a piece or two of herself behind in the process.

But she wasn't about to go back and look for them.

Like Sylvia, she needed to look to the future, and that future did not include a certain hunky trauma surgeon no matter how much she might wish otherwise.

And she didn't wish it. She had a full, satisfying life with her job and crocheting blankets for the center.

She blinked. Wow, when she put it like that, it made her sound kind of sad and lonely, like she had no social life at all.

She didn't. Not really. Not since her divorce, which had left her wary of dating… and relationships in general. She'd invited two men into her life, neither of which had been willing to stick around for her. One of those men was in this car.

"Penny for your thoughts."

"Ha! They're not worth that much." Even if Sylvia wasn't in the car, there was no way she was going to admit she'd been thinking about him.

"I doubt that, but I won't press."

She glanced at him, and despite just having "known" him quite thoroughly, the sight of him still stirred up waters that were best left undisturbed. She doubted that would ever change. She was attracted to him. Probably always would be.

There she went again, letting her thoughts wander all over him.

That doesn't have sexual overtones at all, Maura.

She looked away from him, rolling her eyes and forcing them to stay on the road in front of them.

And there was the center. Just in time.

A woman stood at the front window holding a child. Probably Weston, although she couldn't tell with the glare of the sun. Dex pulled around back and quickly found a parking place.

He glanced back at Sylvia. "Do they have a wheelchair inside?"

"I can walk. I might just be a little slower than most folks."

"You can take all the time you need."

Maura hoped he was including her in that sentence. Because right now she was a little slower than most folks, too. Only hers had nothing to do with her physical health and everything to do with her emotional health.

They managed to get out of the car and, with Sylvia in between them, they slowly made their way up the front walk. By the time they reached the door the woman was out of breath.

"Are you sure you're up to this?"

"Yes. I'll be fine. I can't heal if I'm worried about my son."

She had a point. Maybe Weston would be the healing tonic Sylvia needed—the hope for that future Maura had mentioned.

"I'll get the door." Maura stepped forward and pulled it open so they could go through. She heard the squeal of a child behind her.

"Mommy! Mommy!" She turned in time to see the woman who was holding Weston let him lean forward to hug Sylvia around the neck.

"Easy," the helper said. "Remember, Mommy has some ouchies."

"Ouchie, Mommy?" Weston seemed to look his mother over, searching for these mysterious boo-boos.

"Yes, Mommy has a couple of ouchies." She wrapped her fingers around her son's chin and drew him closer so she could give him a kiss.

He held out a crumpled paper. "For you."

"Thank you, baby." She glanced at the paper. "What did you draw?"

He pointed at one of the scribbled blobs and then the other. "Daddy and Mommy."

Sylvia's hand immediately covered her mouth and tears filled her eyes. "Oh, God, what have I done?"

Maura moved close to her and touched her hand. "What you have done is the right thing for your son. And you."

"Are you sure?" Her unsteady voice was a testament to the pain going through her.

"Absolutely. It was the only thing you could have done. *He* chose this. Not you. Remember that."

Sylvia took a deep breath and nodded, looking back at her son. "Thank you. I love the picture."

The woman holding Weston said, "Let's go back to your room and get you settled. I'll stay there for a while, and then I'll take Weston somewhere to play."

"Thank you."

With that the trio were gone, leaving Maura with Dex. She racked her brain for something to say that wouldn't seem flip after what had just happened and came up empty.

Just then Colleen Winters came out to save the day. "Hi." She shook Dex's hand and gave Maura a quick hug. "I'm so glad you've agreed to teach the first aid class, and I'm really excited to hear what the hospital has planned for our moms."

And just like that, the subject moved to things that had nothing to do with broken hearts or failed relationships. If Maura was very lucky, it would stay that way.

CHAPTER SIX

MAURA WAS TALKING to Matt Foster, the same paramedic he'd seen hanging around the ER several times. Okay…hanging around was probably not the right word for it, since it was normally in conjunction with bringing patients in. And EMTs, by virtue of their profession, often got to know the emergency room crews at the hospitals they normally went to.

This wasn't the first time he'd seen the man conversing with Maura, although that meant nothing. But there was a glimpse of something in the guy's eyes that he recognized. Because he'd once had that very same look when he talked to Maura.

Well, she deserved to be happy. And if Matt did that for her…

She had sex with you, Dex.

Sex they'd both agreed meant nothing. Nothing at all.

If anything, he should be glad, because it meant she wasn't placing her hopes on something that had meant…nothing. And hell if he wasn't suddenly throwing that word around as if he could convince himself of that very thing.

He didn't have to convince himself. It was true.

He took a few steps closer and cleared his throat. Matt looked up first and immediately stopped leaning against the nurse's desk, giving Dex a friendly smile.

But not nearly as friendly as the one he'd given Maura a minute or two ago.

Her head came up a second later, albeit with what seemed like a lot more reluctance.

She'd known it was him and wasn't nearly as glad to see him as she'd been to see the EMT. Damn.

Her smile disappeared, and she suddenly seemed unsure of herself. He hated that. Hated that his presence took away the happy demeanor she'd had a moment ago and replaced it with a wariness that was for him alone. "Hi, Dex. Did we have another meeting planned for today?"

"No, but I thought I'd come down and see if you were free." He didn't say what he'd hoped she was free to do, and as if Matt suddenly realized what was going on, he gave a quick wave. "See you later, Maura?"

"Of course." She flashed him a smile that wasn't real this time, waiting until he left before turning her attention back to Dex.

"What's going on?"

"Just thought I'd check in about the party and what your thoughts were now that we've gotten the center's approval."

"My thoughts about...?"

Okay, so he'd just been headed in to work and hadn't really come here to look for her. Matt's presence had changed his mind.

And that made him angry. At himself.

"About gifts and decorations. You told me you had some ideas but wanted to wait until after the meeting with Colleen to tell me about them."

"Oh, okay. *Those* thoughts." Her muscles seemed to relax. "Well, as you heard, Weston like giraffes. I'd like to see what each of the kids like and get them something geared toward that. Plus a couple of extra things for kids that might arrive over the holidays. And as far as decorations, maybe just the standard. The center puts up a tree, and they normally have a modest party where they sing Christmas carols and have refreshments. What I was thinking was that a traditional party could turn maudlin if we're not careful. I'd like to shift it over a bit so they can forget their problems, if only for a night."

She glanced up at him. "I know this might sound corny, but what if we turned Christmas into a Christmas Hoedown, complete with square dancing and the like. The women could dance with their kids or with each other."

"You know how to square-dance?"

"Well, not so much square dancing, but I've line danced before. How hard could it be?"

How hard, indeed. But he liked the sound of it. It would be hard to dwell on whatever hard situation you were facing if you were kept too busy to think about it. He could imagine a lot of laughter as people tried to

navigate the directions given by the guy calling out dance instructions.

"I like it. I think I know where we can
get some bales of straw, though I have no
idea who to contact about arranging a square
dance."

Like magic, Maura produced a pamphlet
from a deep pocket in her sweater and held
it out to him.

"Square Dancers R Us." He looked up with
a laugh. "Are you kidding me?"

"Nope. Everything you ever wanted to
know about square dancing. And a few things
you didn't."

"So you really did have an idea up your
sleeve. The hospital administration put the
right person in charge of this, I'll give them
that."

Up went her brows. "I thought *you* were
in charge."

And just like that, the mood between them
switched from the heavy cloudiness of the last
week to a much brighter, sunnier day.

"Of a hoedown? Not my forte."

"Mine, either, but it'll be fun, don't you
think? And this way the ladies won't just sit

around sharing war stories, not that I think the center's parties were anything less than warm and caring. But sometimes that can get cloying, if overdone. Can bring back memories that are best left in the past."

Like memories of them? Together?

Not the time, Dex.

"You're right. I think a hoedown is perfect, and with a place like this—" he waved the pamphlet "—what could go wrong?"

"My thoughts exactly. I told them I'd need to talk to you first, but they actually offered to come talk to us. Together."

"Here at the hospital?" He hoped so. Or at the center. Or anywhere else except her house. Because he knew if they went there it would happen again, despite his repeated lectures to himself. One look at that sofa and the memories would doom him to a Groundhog Day–type scenario that repeated again and again and again. And while having sex with her over and over and over might seem like a dream come true, with it came the bad stuff. Consequences that weren't nearly as fun as what led up to them.

"Yes. I asked the hospital administrator if

we could use one of the conference rooms, and he said yes."

About a hundred muscles relaxed at once. "Great. When is this meeting?"

"I told them I'd need to check with you about your schedule. Any idea when you'll be free?"

He thought for a minute. "I have surgery every day except for weekends and evenings. How about you?"

"I have this Saturday free, but that doesn't give us much time to pull it all together."

"How about this? If the company doesn't have a date before Christmas free, we can still decorate with straw bales and do a country-and-western-themed event."

"Can you be our caller?"

"Um…no. My knowledge of square dancing is *Swing your partner and promenade*. Beyond that I'm pretty much clueless."

"Oh, really?" She grinned and flipped a strand of hair backward. Before he could stop it, the image of those dark wavy locks tumbling across her naked back came screaming through his head. His mouth went dry as the events of that night swirled around him. His body took that as an invitation to start preparations. In quick order.

Dammit. He needed to knock this off before she realized exactly what his brain was working on. And it had nothing to do with Christmas parties or square dances. "So Saturday? Will they meet with us on a weekend?"

"Let me check and see—while the ER is quiet."

She held her hand out. It took a second to realize that she wasn't asking him to hold her hand. She just wanted the pamphlet. He gave it to her.

Glancing at the front of it, she took her phone out of her pocket and dialed. She waited for a second, then started talking. "So the other member of the committee can meet on Saturday. Would that work?"

Of course she didn't ask him if he had plans for this Saturday, but since he hadn't prefaced his days off with any activities, she couldn't be blamed for assuming.

"Eight o'clock?" She glanced at him, seeking his thought. When he nodded, she told whoever was on the other end of the line that

that would work. "The conference room is on the third floor at the very end of the hallway. It's conference room one."

She paused and then said, "Great, see you then." Then she ended the call.

"Are you sure that time is okay with you?"

"Yep, or I would have said something."

She bit her lip. "Well, okay. Thanks then."

He couldn't stand it any longer. "Hey, thanks for doing this with me. I'm sure it's awkward after…that night. But thanks for not backing out. I think your idea will be a lot of fun and will mean a lot to the residents."

"I hope so. And I could say the same thing about you. I know this can't be easy. But it was a fluke. A remnant of the past that caught up with us." She tilted her head. "I've thought a lot about what happened. I don't think either of us got the closure we might have needed. I know I didn't. So maybe that's what part of it was all about. Getting closure."

Closure. That had an air of finality he didn't like. But what could he say? *Screw the closure and let's go into conference room one where we can have a meeting of our own? Just the two of us?*

Not hardly. And he did his best not to re-visit the past any more than he had to. That led only to pain, whether the past was related to his family or to Maura. It helped nothing. And it made life harder.

He'd proved that on her couch.

"Maybe you're right," he said. "The past is the past. Sometimes you just have to make sure it stays there."

Her head snapped back, and she blinked a couple of times before responding. "Yes. You're right. It's up to us to make sure that happens. If you're worried about me, don't be. I have no intention of sliding back there for another visit. What's done is done. Thank you for reminding me of that."

Hell, he hadn't been trying to remind *her* of anything. He'd been trying to remind himself. He seemed to have screwed that up some-how, and he didn't know how to right it or if he even should.

So he did the one thing he seemed to be good at. He finished off the conversation as quickly as he could and said goodbye, stroll-ing down the hallway without a single glance behind him. Once inside the safety of the elevator, he looked at the ceiling and shook his head.

"Way to go, Dex. Yet another witty rejoinder tumbles off the cliff."

All he knew was that this was the last time he was going to chase a man away from Maura Findley. And that's what it had been. He'd seen Matt talking to her and had barged over there like some jealous husband. What had it gotten him? A scheduled meeting and being told by that same woman that sex with him was her way of slamming the book shut on him.

The only problem was that he wasn't sure he liked it being closed.

They ended up changing the meeting place. After talking to the Square Dancers R Us people, it dawned on Maura that she was leaving the most important people out of this particular conversation: the women at the shelter. They, more than anyone, deserved to have a say in what kind of party they wanted. So an hour before the square dance people were supposed to come, Maura and Dex were in the cafeteria area of the center, meeting with the thirteen women who were housed there, along with their kids, who played in a corner or were held on their mothers' laps. Dex had asked her to take the lead, so she stood in front of them, laid out what they had done so far and asked for the consensus.

"I really like it." Sylvia spoke up. "I've never square-danced before, but it would be fun to learn. Although I might not be as agile as I normally would be."

Her throat tightened. Sylvia was still healing from her ordeal.

"It's not about being agile or perfect. It's about being able to laugh and have fun with people who have been in similar circumstances."

Was that what she and Dex were? People who had shared similar circumstances?

It wasn't quite the same thing. And not everything about her and Dex's relationship had been bad. Some of it had been sweet and good…and perfect. Even their time on her couch?

Well, that didn't count, because they weren't in a relationship anymore.

Several more women spoke up, and all of

them were in favor of the hoedown. "The kids would like it, too. I wonder what those fake bulls cost? The kind that twist and turn and you fall off. I bet the kids would love that."

"That's a great idea." Maura scribbled the idea in the notebook she'd brought with her. The hospital had pretty much given them carte blanche as far as costs went, so a bucking bull probably wouldn't break the bank. She glanced around the room. It wasn't huge, but put some tables up front with a Christmas meal, which would be served buffet style, and line the walls with straw bales for people to sit on and eat or watch the square dancers in the middle, and it would be fairly simple to transform this place into something out of the ordinary. Especially with a fake rodeo bull for the kids to climb on and try to ride.

Dex was sitting two rows back on the end, watching her. There was something in his eye that made her go warm all over. Hopefully, her face wasn't beet red in response. But this was turning out to be a lot of fun. If someone had told her a year ago, she'd be planning a square dance with her high school sweetheart she'd have said they were crazy. And maybe she was the crazy one for letting herself get roped into this. Still, it didn't feel crazy. At least not right now.

She'd thought that sex with him was a bad thing, that it had shown her to be weak. But maybe not. Maybe this could be a whole new start for them. Not as boyfriend and girlfriend, instead as friends. The place they'd been many, many years ago, before their first kiss in the snow.

She liked that. Liked the idea that they didn't have to be mortal enemies or avoid speaking to each other. Maybe there was a happy medium.

"Dex, do you have any thoughts you want to share?"

He leaned back in his seat. "That I want to share? I don't think anyone wants to hear those." He glanced at his watch. "I think the event planners are due here in a few minutes. Maybe we can break for refreshments."

They'd set up some cookies and juice. Maura was relieved that they hadn't rolled their eyes at the thought of a hoedown. Instead, she'd caught glimpses of excitement in their eyes. And for a group of women who didn't have a lot to get excited about, she was thrilled that the hospital was providing this for them.

While the women took their kids to the table to get snacks, Dex came over to her and bumped her shoulder. "Good job."

"I think they're happy about it, don't you?"

"I do." He gave her a smile. "The only thing I'm worried about is finding a mechanical bull."

She laughed. "I know, right? But I really want to find something, if possible."

"How about if I work on that?"

"Seriously?" She laughed. "Are you going to try them out to find the best one?"

"Can you see me on a bull?" His widening grin made her shiver. It had been so long since they'd been able to joke back and forth like this. It felt good. A little too good.

"I'm picturing it right now, but I'd need to see a video to be sure."

"That will never happen."

"You know what they say about never, don't you?" She tilted her head to look at him. This was one man who was easy on the eye, which was probably why she found herself staring at him more than she liked.

"I'm probably better off not knowing."

"Well, I'll take you up on finding the bull, if you're serious about looking for one."

"I'll do it."

Sylvia came over, holding Weston's hand, and said to Maura, "I just wanted to say thanks again for all you did for me." She glanced around the room. "And for all of us."

"It's really the hospital that's doing it."

She gave Maura a look. "None of this would have happened without you."

"Well, Dex is the one who presented a proposal for something, and the hospital offered to fund a party. So none of it would have happened without him."

"Well, thanks to both of you. This is going to mean so much to our kids. And us." She put a hand on her son's head. "It's been really hard with everything that's happened. I feel so terrible. If someone other than me would have walked out of the center at that exact time, he could have hurt or killed someone else."

"That's not on you, Sylvia. It's on him.

Have you talked to someone about it?" Survivor's guilt was a very real thing.

"We have a counselor here, so yes. We've talked. And it's helped a lot."

She saw a sudden flash of fear appear in Sylvia's eyes, and she drew Weston close to her side. Maura looked out the window in time to see two men getting out of a white van, which had a company logo emblazoned on the back doors.

She touched the other woman's hand. "It's just the men from the square dancing place."

"Oh, okay." She looked embarrassed, although it was a natural reaction. "I'll go get Weston another snack before we get started."

Maura's heart ached. Sylvia's life was forever changed. And each of the women in this room probably had a similar story, each manifesting their trauma in different ways.

And Dex's trauma. How had it manifested? Oh, she'd been an eyewitness to the changes his loss had wrought, and they hadn't been pretty. And his hadn't been the only life that had been changed. Hers had, too.

She sat while the men from Square Dancers R Us presented their ideas for the party.

This time Maura was able to sit and observe reactions among those in the room and, like Dex had said, there were nodding heads and smiles. One of the women raised her hand. "What if I have two left feet?"

There was laughter at that remark, and a couple of other women voiced similar concerns.

"It's not a matter of knowing how to move when, but enjoying the process."

Maura liked that explanation. Maybe that's what she and Dex needed to do. Enjoy the process of becoming friends again.

Unless that wasn't what he wanted. Although she got the feeling he was at least open to it.

The meeting ended on a good note and they agreed on a date. December 23, which was on a Wednesday evening. With a little less than two weeks to go, it was cutting it a bit close, but the event planner was handling the dancing itself and would provide all the speakers and microphones.

And there would even be costumes!

Maura had been thrilled to hear that they were going to bring a wardrobe of all kinds of fun things from neck scarves to the bouffant skirts worn by square dancers. They could wear as much or as little of it as they wanted.

Riding back with Dex, she leaned her head on the leather headrest, letting the darkness outside of the vehicle wash over her. His scent surrounded her, clung to her, slid inside of her with each and every breath.

Right now there was no place she'd rather be.

She'd better not let herself get too comfortable, though, because every time she let her guard down with this man, something happened. Sometimes good. Sometimes sad. And one time it had been horrible, like when she'd lost his baby and felt like the very last part of Dex had slipped away from her forever.

Her grief had been paralyzing even though the pregnancy was early, still in her first trimester. To have gone from the heights of joy when she learned she was carrying his baby to what she thought was the lowest of lows when she realized he didn't want to move forward with their relationship. Then she'd discovered there was something even worse than that. Worse than anything she'd experienced thus far in her life.

Gabe hadn't wanted children at all. For some reason, she'd been just fine with that, convincing herself that she didn't want them, either, that she'd dodged a bullet with the other pregnancy. But it was all a lie. Being with Dex again had made her realize that. She did want a child. Even if she had to do it on her own. Once this Christmas party was over, she was going to start the year with a brand-new resolution. She was going to be a mom, whether that meant having a biological child or adopting one. She'd been in a holding pattern for a long, long time, maybe even since before her marriage. Maybe that was ultimately what had done it in. But no more. She was going to move forward with her life once and for all. And to her, that meant having a child of her own.

"Are you asleep over there?"

She blinked her thoughts away and turned her head toward him. "Nope. Just happy with how the night went."

"Me, too. And I was just thinking about

something." He glanced over at her. "How tired are you?"

"Not very, why?"

One of his brows went up, and he gave her a slow smile. One that made heat pool in the center of her belly and brought up visions of the last time they were together.

"Are you up for some excitement?" he murmured.

She licked her lips. "Haven't you had enough, um, excitement for one night?"

"Not quite. I told myself I'd do this on my own, but some things are more fun when done as a pair."

"As a pair?"

"Yes. I think I have the perfect thing to close out tonight, Maura." He reached over and twirled a strand of her hair, tugging it and sending shivers up and down her spine. "But only if you're ready to take a wild ride. One of the wildest you've ever had."

CHAPTER SEVEN

A BAR. HE'D brought her to a bar.

He pulled to a stop and aimed that stinkin' cute grin at her.

She laughed. Oh, hell, she'd thought he was talking about doing something a little naughtier than buying drinks. She'd been taking stock of what undergarments she had on, just in case.

She should be relieved. Very relieved that he'd chosen something completely innocuous.

"So what are we doing here?"

"Research." He swung out of the car and came around to her side before she could get her seat belt off, opening the door for her.

Was he kidding her? "Research?"

Climbing out of her car, she waited for him to close the door.

"It will all become clear in a minute."

She'd never been to this particular bar before, not that she had ever been a big bar hopper, even in her younger, wilder days. Back in high school, she'd had Dex, and that had been the only high she'd needed. The only thing she'd wanted.

And thinking about that did no good at all.

Dex reached the door to the bar and waited for her to catch up before saying, "Ready?"

"I think so, but at this point I'm not positive." She really had no idea what he had in mind.

He swung the door open and what greeted her was noise. And flashing lights. And someone being tossed around by a…bull.

Not a real bull. A mechanical bull.

"Oh, my God! Really?" She laughed, struggling to catch her breath. "A wild ride, huh? I should have known."

He gave her a sideways look, his own smile completely guileless. "What did you think I was talking about?"

That fake innocence gave him away. "Well, I knew you weren't talking about *that*. Because *wild* isn't the term I would use for…

well…you know. In fact, that was pretty darn—"

"Don't even go there, Maura. My pride can only take so much." But his own laugh made her relax.

There was no way she was going to tell him that he really was the wildest she'd ever had. And the best. It made her feel bad for Gabe, but Dex truly had set the bar pretty damn high.

"Well, let's go see what this bull has to offer. Maybe they can at least tell us where we can rent one."

Dex somehow located a table in the crowded space and then ordered two beers, bringing them to her. She took one and lifted her glass to take a big sip as she watched the main attraction: the bull, which was evidently between rounds.

"Who's next?" someone called over the loudspeaker. "Two minutes on Bubba gets you a free beer. Which you're gonna need after taking this big boy on." Laughter filled the room, and someone stood and swaggered over to the big bull, which was complete with his own set of horns. Maura hoped those things weren't as real as they looked. A nasty gore would be something even a free beer couldn't fix. She made a note to make sure whatever bull they rented was sans horns, or at least had them made out of foam.

The guy climbed on, and someone motioned for him to hold on to what looked like a strap of some kind. There was cushioned material all around the perimeter for obvious reasons.

"Ready?"

The man gave a thumbs-up and the bull started up. Nice and slow. An easy back-and-forth motion was followed by a leisurely quarter turn, which the guy rode with ease.

"Well, that doesn't look too hard."

The gentle movements continued for another thirty seconds or so. At this rate, the guy was going to win a beer for sure. As if on a timer, though, a raucous country song started blasting through the speakers and the bull suddenly lurched forward while making another quarter turn. The crowd had evidently been waiting for this moment, whooping it up with catcalls and yelling for him to ride it out. The motions became jerkier and without a defined direction, one time doing a 180-degree turn. The man was actually doing an admirable job clinging to the machine. Another fast turn and a leap into the air was followed by twist to the left, and that did it. The guy went sailing into the cushioned wall, before leaping to his feet and pumping his fist into the air.

"One minute thirty seconds. Almost made it, folks. Give him a round of applause. And we're ready for a new victim…er… I mean contender."

She turned to Dex. "How did you even know this place existed?" It didn't exactly look like the kind of place he would hang out in. Then again, it had been a long time and maybe he'd changed.

He held up his phone. "I did a quick Google search when a mechanical bull was mentioned at our meeting. I thought it might be good to see one in action before we decide it's right for the party."

"Good idea. It looks like they can control how fast it goes. The kids would definitely like it, if we can get one that is made for fun. Not sure how many of the moms would ride it."

"Well, our patient definitely shouldn't try it, even with a little more healing time under her belt."

The next person climbed on the bull and had the same result, only he didn't make it quite as long.

"I used to ride horses when I was younger, but they definitely don't move like that. At least not the ones I rode," she said.

A spotlight spun around the room and found a third participant who wasn't quite as eager to go up but, with a little coaxing from the crowd, finally did. This person, a young man in a suit, of all things, got the kid-glove treatment. The person controlling the thing kept things light and easy until around the minute and forty-five-second mark when, without warning, the person seemed to simply slide down the side of the bull and drop to the ground. "Okay, well I think even I could have ridden that one."

As if someone in the audience had heard her, the spotlight suddenly picked her out of the crowd and held on. Horror swept over her, and she tried to shake her head even as the crowd started chanting. "Ride that bull, ride that bull…"

"Did you tell them to choose me?"

Dex leaned back, placing his hand over his heart. "I swear, I had nothing to do with it. But if you want a real test…"

"I am going to kill you." Maybe it was the beer, although she hadn't even ingested half of it. Maybe it was having Dex look at her in that expectant, challenging way, but she did something she never could have seen herself doing a year or two ago. She got up from her chair and walked toward the center of the room, where the bull waited. It was bigger than she expected, and the floor was more bouncy than padded. Kind of like a trampoline. Someone came up to her and showed her a raised padded platform that she could use to hop onto the bull's back.

What in the world was she thinking? But she climbed up and waited as the man showed her how to hold on. What she'd thought was a strap was actually a thick piece of rope with a wooden bead on it. "Hold here. Try to go with the movements of the bull as much as possible, using your other hand for balance. When you're ready to go, hold your hand up."

When she was ready? Well, that would be never. Taking a deep breath and glancing at the table where Dex had been, she was disappointed to see it was empty. He couldn't even be bothered to stay and watch her? Maybe an emergency call had come in and he'd had to go.

Well, it didn't matter, and she might as well get this over with. Raising her hand in the air, she gave the signal. The bull started with slow, gentle motions, just like with everyone else.

Okay, it really wasn't too bad. She did half a twist and saw Dex right there beside the ring, watching her. Then he was gone as the bull moved in another direction. The action picked up a bit, but it still wasn't too hard. Until a quick turn almost unseated her. She regained her balance, but the movements were becoming too unpredictable and it was all she could do to stay on. *Go with the movements.* Way easier said than done.

Hadn't she already passed the two-minute mark? It felt like she'd been going forever.

The bull shimmied, then spun. And that was the end. She felt herself falling before she even realized what was happening, and then bouncing on the springy floor.

She laughed. It actually was fun.

"One minute thirty-five seconds for the lady. Good job!"

"Yes. Good job." A hand came down to help her to her feet. She grabbed it, thinking it was the helper who'd instructed her when she got on, but it was Dex. When her eyes met his, they shimmered with something that could have been admiration.

She took a step and then tumbled against him. "Whew, I'm a little bit dizzy. Or maybe a little tipsy."

He held her in place, hands on her hips. Something went very warm inside of her. Especially when he seemed in no hurry to let go.

"It's probably the surface, it's hard to walk on." Then he moved, his arm curving around her waist to help her walk away from the area. "I can't believe you did it."

Once she got to the regular floor, it was easier going, but she still had a slight sense of vertigo.

"I can't believe I did, either. I looked over and thought you'd left."

"I was going to try to give you moral support, but they didn't have you facing my way very often."

She laughed. "I saw you. Right before they flipped me the other way."

"So, what's the verdict? Yes, for the party? Or no?"

"I say yes. The older kids will have a lot of fun with it and the younger ones…well, maybe there's a way to help them stay on."

"Most rental places send someone with the bull to operate it. I'm sure."

She put a hand to her ear and kind of yanked it away again, as she shook her head. "Wow, that really did a number on the otoconia crystals in my ear."

"I bet. Did you fix it?"

Maura peered around. "Yes, that's better." Otoconia crystals, which helped with balance could cause vertigo when displaced. Her mom had had problems with them, and she'd learned techniques on how to reposition them so they no longer interfered with balance. But she'd never had to use it on herself.

She took another sip of her beer and watched as the next lucky contestant got on the bull. "Sure you don't want to try it?"

"Believe me, I was right up there with you. Right until you crashed to the ground. Unlike you, I didn't ride anything that wasn't motorized as a kid, other than a bike. I think I would have been off on that first turn. But I'll admit to liking the way you rode him."

Something about the last sentence made her flush, because all she could think about was the way she'd ridden something that was a lot more cooperative than that bull.

Dex finished off his beer. "That's it for me, since I need to drive, but I'll get you another if you want."

"Nope, I'm good. I've always been a lightweight."

"Yes, you have." He chuckled. "We did some pretty stupid stuff back then."

"We did. I remember going down to that creek behind my house and using a flashlight to hunt for crawdads at night."

He ran a finger along the line of her jaw. "Hunting for crawdads wasn't all we did."

No, it wasn't. Dex had been her first, and she'd always believed he'd be her last.

But she wasn't going to ruin a nice night out by dwelling on that. "We had some fun times."

"Yes, we did."

He threw a couple bills on the table and stood. "Ready?"

"I am."

Dex started the car and backed out of the space. He couldn't believe she'd gotten on that bull. The Maura he'd known as a kid would have been one of the first to raise her hand and volunteer. This Maura, the fully grown adult woman, had changed in some undecipherable ways. There were times she seemed a little more unsure of herself than she used to be. Was that because of her marriage? Because of him?

"How's your ear?"

"All better. But I probably won't repeat that anytime soon. One time on a bull was enough for me. I'll leave that for the rodeo stars and the bar warriors." She laughed. "I should have realized something was going on when I looked at the bar's name. Just The Bull. Catchy."

"No catchier than Square Dancers R Us."

"Touché."

She leaned her head against the headrest. "Thanks for tonight. I think I needed a night out."

"It's been a while for me, too." It had been. Being involved with the women's center and this party were just what he needed. And Maura?

No. That had been settled a long time ago. He wouldn't go back and undo it, even if he could. They would have ended up in a divorce court the same way she and her husband had. He'd been a mess back then. He still was in a lot of ways. He told himself every winter that once his mom was gone, he was moving to Florida. Or South Texas, or anywhere that had no snowfall.

But while he'd recovered from what had happened—for the most part—his mom had not. She'd struggled for a long time before finally receiving a diagnosis and treatment for clinical depression. Dex had not been able to help her through any of it, because he'd been too busy just trying to keep his own head above water. Looking back, he hadn't done a very good job of that, either. He'd called and visited plenty of times since the accident, but maybe it was time to call her and have a hard talk about what had happened and what they each hoped from the future.

If he'd done that with Maura, would they still be where they were now? It was too late for recriminations now. She'd moved on, and maybe he could finally do the same.

As if the universe had overheard his thoughts and decided to test his resolve, a big flake of snow landed on the windshield, then another and another. Soon the snowfall increased. Not bad, but enough that his hands gripped the steering wheel, eyes searching for any irregularities in the vehicles around him.

He shouldn't have had that beer.

No, that was ridiculous. He was well under the legal limit and that single drink had been spaced out over the course of an hour, so much of it was already metabolized.

A hand touched his arm. "Hey, want me to drive?"

She knew. When he glanced at his knuckles, he saw why. They were white. He forced his fingers to loosen their grip.

Everything in him wanted to take her up

on her offer, but his pride said no way. "I'm fine. Traffic is pretty light right now."

He drove to work in the snow every damn winter, so why couldn't he get over this? Maybe for the same reason his mom still struggled. Another reason to call her.

"Are you sure? I don't mind. I know this used to be hard for you."

It still was. And back then, he actually had let Maura take over on occasion, but it had always rankled that he just couldn't seem to get his act together. On anything, including his relationship with her. With his mom.

"We're almost there, anyway. Just another five minutes." He cast around for something to say that would divert her attention to something else. "Do you and your ex keep in touch?"

"Gabe?" Her head swiveled toward him. "No. Why do you ask?"

"No reason. I was just curious." He wasn't about to tell her the real reason for the change in topic, but he'd obviously chosen the wrong one.

"There's not really anything to tie us together anymore. We don't have kids."

So maybe her miscarriage was like his aversion to snow? A trauma that had led her to avoid trying to have more?

He reached the hospital parking garage and she told him where her car was parked. "I'm sorry about that. You were really good with Sylvia's little boy."

"Thanks. I've been thinking lately that I might want kids."

A shaft of pain went through him at the thought of her having babies with someone else, but he forced himself to nod as if he understood. "I'm sure getting over your miscarriage was hard."

"You have no idea."

Dex found her car and pulled in beside it. "How long had you been married when it happened?"

There was a huge pause. Maura picked at a spot on her slacks before finally replying.

"Gabe and I weren't together when it happened."

His brain stuttered and stopped. Had there been someone in between the time he and Maura broke up and when she got together with her husband? It had only been a year, and it had almost killed him when he'd heard she was getting married. He'd almost stormed the church and been the single dissenting voice. But he hadn't. Because he had no right. He couldn't tell her that he wanted to slow things down and then expect she would just be fine with it. He'd subconsciously known she wouldn't, which was why he'd done what he did.

"I didn't realize you dated someone else after we broke up."

She shifted in her seat to look at him, her lips tightening. "Who said I dated someone else?"

"Well…" Maybe that beer really had affected him, because what she was saying made no sense at all.

"That baby…the one I lost…" Her chin tilted in defiance. "It was yours."

"Mine?" His paralyzed brain lurched forward, unseating him just like that mechanical bull had done with its victims less than an hour ago. He was missing something. Something big. He struggled to make it out, his mind going back over what had happened on the last day they were together.

One thing he was very sure of—she'd never mentioned being pregnant when she'd talked to him. "The baby was mine?"

She nodded but didn't say anything.

His mind slid down an ugly path. He paused before putting to words the question that pounded inside of him. "Did you know about it before you broke things off with me?"

"Does it matter? It doesn't change anything."

It did matter. A lot. He just wasn't sure why. He'd dealt with so much loss that last year, and to find out after all this time that he'd lost a child, as well…

A baby. *His* baby.

Raw pain boiled through his system, searing places he hadn't realized existed.

No. She wouldn't have kept something like that from him. She must have found out about the pregnancy after they broke up.

What if she hadn't lost it? Would she have gone through with carrying the baby to term and never told him the child was his? Or worse, let Gabe raise the child as his?

His jaw clenched as he worked to contain

his emotions. "You didn't think I had a right to know I was going to be a father?"

"Believe me, Dex. I absolutely thought you did. But the night I came over to talk to you about it was the night you told me you weren't ready for a commitment." She touched his hand. "If you weren't ready to make a commitment to our relationship, then you definitely weren't ready to hear the news that I was pregnant. And you were still dealing with…so much back then."

Yes, he had been. But that didn't excuse the fact that he would have wanted to know the truth. He'd deserved to know. "Hell, Maura. If you'd told me up front, before demanding to know where you stood, things might have been different."

"Really? You seriously believe that?" She shook her head. "Even if that were the case, I didn't want you under those conditions. Didn't want that for our child. So when I realized you were probably never going to be ready, were never going to be able to get past what happened to your family, I broke it off. And from where I'm sitting, it looks like you never did."

Was she talking about the fact that he was still a nervous wreck when driving in the snow? Or was she referring to the fact that he'd never gotten married?

He could be flip and say he'd never met the right woman. But that would be a lie. Because he had. He just hadn't been able to give her what she wanted back then. And honestly, he didn't think if she'd asked him to commit two years later or ten years later, it would have made any difference. He'd liked his life the way it was. When he'd only needed to worry about himself, not anyone else.

And if he'd known about the baby? Would that have forced him to think about something other than his own sad circumstances?

He didn't know because he hadn't had the chance to decide that.

As angry as that made him, he could still see her point. She hadn't wanted a marriage proposal based on the pregnancy. If she had, she certainly could have played that card and gotten what she wanted. But he knew Maura well enough to realize it was all or nothing. She would not settle for half measures. And she shouldn't have had to. He took a couple of deep breaths and said the one thing he absolutely knew was true.

"I'm sorry you went through all of that alone."

One of her shoulders lifted. "It's over. And losing the baby was probably for the best."

For the best.

Goddammit. How could she even think that? He closed his eyes for a few seconds. He'd done a number on her. Had hurt her in ways that were unimaginable. She probably did think it was for the best. If he'd been in her shoes, he probably would have done the same. He might have even ended the pregnancy.

He was glad she hadn't, even though she'd lost the baby anyway.

They were wild and crazy back when they were together, had done some sexy, risky things, but they'd always used protection. Every single time. Evidently something had gone wrong during one of their lovemaking sessions, and she'd gotten pregnant.

The word stuck in his brain like a claw. She'd been carrying his child, and he'd never had a chance to celebrate that fact…or grieve its loss.

He reached over and captured her hand. "I'm so sorry, Maura. So very sorry." He wasn't sure how to express himself without insulting her. "I hope you know I would have tried to do the right thing. Would have wanted to be in the baby's life, if he or she had survived. I wouldn't have left you to do everything on your own."

He thought of Sylvia and how she would be raising Weston on her own because of her husband's selfishness.

"I just didn't know what to do back then. I was hurt and sad, and the last thing I wanted to do was burden you with something else. All I wanted to do was get away." She squeezed his hand. "But I think after I'd had time to sift through my feelings, I would have done the right thing, too, and told you that you were going to be a father."

Well, they were a mess. Even now. Dex wasn't sure how to compartmentalize the sudden revelation or if he even could. His whole reason for breaking up with her had been because he couldn't deal with any more losses and the realization that there was no way to guarantee something wouldn't eventually happen to Maura, as well. It had all been too much.

No wonder she'd steered away from the topic back then. She probably figured it wouldn't change anything for him to know, so she'd simply kept the information to herself.

She said if she hadn't lost the baby she probably would have eventually told him. He needed to try to be content with that. "Thank you for telling me now."

"I wasn't going to, you know. Not after all this time. I'm not even sure why I did."

"Well, I'm glad you did." He took a deep breath, before giving her hand one last squeeze and releasing it. "You're going to make a great mom."

But it wouldn't be to his baby. And that thought made something shift in his chest.

She unlatched her seat belt and popped open her door. "I hope so. When the time is right."

And then she got out of the car and into her own. He stayed where he was as she started the vehicle and pulled out of the space, giving a quick wave as she drove away.

And still he sat there, his emotions and thoughts in absolute turmoil.

Maura had been expecting his child, and he'd had absolutely no idea.

CHAPTER EIGHT

MUCH OF THEIR dealings in the time leading up to the Christmas party had been via text message.

Maura hadn't wanted to tell him about the pregnancy, especially after all this time, but having him assume she'd had a boyfriend right on the heels of their breakup had made her angry.

He had no idea what she'd gone through back then. The devastation and overwhelming pain that had come from knowing he hadn't wanted her. And then when she'd told him the baby wasn't Gabe's—for him to have thought she could just jump into another man's arms and gotten pregnant by that person...

Well, it had sent her over the edge and the words had come pouring out. She'd wanted them to slice into him, the way his veiled accusation had cut into her.

After the anger, though, came hurt.

But once she'd worked through all that, his reaction to the news had surprised her. Although he'd obviously been upset that she hadn't told him about it back then, he'd also seemed relieved in some indefinable way, although it was the opposite of what she would have expected. If she'd been him, she would have hoped the baby *was* the product of a fling or her marriage, rather than discovering the child was his.

She'd tried to call him a couple of days after their trip to the bar, but then had disconnected when she realized there was really nothing to say. She couldn't go back and undo her decisions, and he couldn't undo his. And as she'd said about the pregnancy, it was for the best.

So how was she going to face him tonight?

The same way she'd faced him any other time. The news didn't change anything between them. Well, maybe it had put paid to the chance to be friends with him. From what she'd seen of his succinct messages that had come over her phone, he wanted as little interaction with her as possible.

Fortunately, the square dancing group had offered to do the decorating, once she'd told them what she wanted. And Colleen Winters used the food budget from the hospital to take care of the meal. That left getting the bull, and Dex had secured one of those, according to one of those text messages.

Some part of her grieved in a way that she hadn't during the loss of her child. She hadn't expected to get back together with Dex, but had hoped for a little more than what they were left with: quick glimpses of him as he traveled through her department.

But it was what it was. She should be used to it by now.

So she got dressed in a pair of dark-washed jeans and a white button-down shirt. Not exactly square dance material, but it was as close to Western wear as she could get. And even though she wasn't in a party mood, she was going to go with an attitude that this wasn't about her—it was about those women. Because it was true. No matter what was going on in her personal life, she wanted those moms and kids to have fun. They deserved a little hope…a glimpse of what life could still be like.

And after her talk with Dex, she had cemented her decision to have a child. It was going to happen. Relationships with men might not have worked out, but she could give a child a good and loving home. And that's all that mattered, in the end.

Brushing her hair and pulling it into a high ponytail, slicking on a bit of lip gloss and a touch of mascara, she looked in the mirror.

Well, that was about as good as it was going to get. Today, anyway. She needed to go and try to have a good time. Or at least paste on a smile and pretend. Ha! The same word she'd tossed at Dex after they'd made love. Gathering up the bags of gifts she'd bought for the kids based on the information the mothers had given them, she headed out the door and into the world.

She got to the center fifteen minutes early and spotted Dex's car already there, along with a box truck with the Square Dancers R Us logo on the side. There was another truck that had probably brought in the bull. Lord, she hoped all that had fit in the center's cafeteria.

But at least there was no snow in sight, for Dex's sake.

Her nerves gave a threatening twinge, taunting her to get back in her car and head down the road. But she'd given her word and that meant more than any discomfort this one night could bring, so she rang the buzzer and waited for someone to answer.

It was Colleen, who gave her a big hug. "I can't believe what they've done to the place. It's magical. And fun."

"Dex did a lot of the legwork." Like taking her to a bar so she could see a mechanical bull in action.

She'd been so hopeful that night.

Well, it wasn't all doom and gloom. Maybe they could get past this, too. Once the shock wore off, maybe Dex would forgive her for keeping her secret. He'd taken it a lot better than she'd expected, but not well enough to call or try to stop in the ER to talk to her.

"I know he did," said the director. "He's helping with the bull now."

"He is?"

"Yep, come on in and see what the hospital's generosity has done for us."

She went in and had to stop and blink at the change in the room. It was just as she'd imagined. No. Even better. Bales of straw lined the perimeter of the room, the way she'd pictured it, but each of those bales had a red ribbon draped from end to end. The bull was set up in a corner, with what looked like a big inflatable pool underneath it. The walls on either side of the bull were padded and the creature's fake horns each had silver tinsel wrapped around them. Kids surrounded the pit, touching and examining the bull, and Dex was holding Weston on the animal's back. The boy even had a tiny cowboy hat perched on his head.

She pressed a palm to her mouth to stop its trembling. Oh, Lord, she was not going to cry. She couldn't.

Long tables were laid out with two big centerpieces and what looked like a whole bevy of slow cookers and food offerings.

Colleen saw her glance and said, "The women decided they were going to cook, so they each made a dish or two."

"What a wonderful idea." It was so important for these women to have a sense of ownership, and their contributions made that happen.

She glanced back at the bull and found Dex's eyes on her. She gave a quick wave, with a smile that felt like it stretched her face to the limit. But what else could she do?

The center of the room had been totally cleared out, and the event company had actually laid out a wooden dance floor in a big octagon. Some of the kids were rolling and playing on it, but when she looked at the people who were still setting up equipment, no one seemed bothered.

So good. This was going to be so very good.

Her muscles relaxed, and she watched Colleen move over to the dessert section of the buffet table, talking to one of the residents about something.

It was now or never. She walked over to the bull. Dex had already lifted Weston down and was helping another kid perch on it. "Hey. Can you believe all this?"

"I can't. The decorations are great. Did you come over and help with them?"

She shook her head. "No, the event company did everything, and it's absolutely amazing. I hope the hospital is okay with giving them a generous tip."

"Already in the works. I made sure of it."

"Great." She glanced around. "I saw Weston, but I haven't seen Sylvia. Is she okay?"

"She was here a few minute ago. She's getting around much better. Her stitches are out, and her wounds are healing well. I saw her last week at the hospital."

And he hadn't called her to let her know. Why would he? She'd had almost no part in the case.

"I'm really glad. How are they going to work the bull?"

"They're going to use the lowest settings. Supposedly even a kid can make it through it. I imagine some of them might fall off on purpose, just for the chance to bounce on the inflatable tubes, though."

Looking closer, she realized that what she'd thought was a pool was actually a network of tubes that hooked into the raised edges, which were the same configuration.

She smiled. "Are you going to ride it this time, since they've ramped it down?"

He gave her a grin. "You never know. Although I imagine the kids are going to be fighting each other to get on it."

Just then the caller took a microphone off the stand and tested it, before giving the greeting. "Welcome to our first annual Christmas Hoedown! We've got some fun things planned and it looks like we've got a couple of wild animals in attendance, as well. And that doesn't include the bull."

Everyone laughed as more and more of the residents came into the room. "If you have any questions, feel free to ask any of us—we'll be scattered around the room. There's a costume rack behind me so feel free to come on over and choose something to wear for the festivities. After all, this is a hoedown. We need to dress the part."

She glanced at Dex and saw that he had on black jeans and a black shirt. The combination suited him. There was no scarf around his powerful neck, but he'd done a pretty good job at fitting into his surroundings.

The caller continued. "I'd like Drs. Dex Chamblisse and Maura Findley to come up here, if they will."

She glanced up at Dex, wondering if he was behind this. He just shrugged. She followed him up to the front and stood beside the man with the microphone, hands clasped tightly in front of her.

"I'd like to thank these two for calling us and giving us the opportunity to come and serve you. It's the opportunity of a lifetime. Most of you don't know this, but..." He paused before reaching up to pinch the top of his nose for several long seconds, as if trying to compose himself. Then he straightened his cowboy hat and looked up. "My daughter was in a position that many of you face right now. She got out and is safe, thanks to an organization very much like this one. She's remarried—to a good man, this time—and is happier than she's ever been. And that's what we all want, isn't it? The chance to be happy?" He cued someone who sat at a nearby sound table, and the sound of a banjo came over the loudspeaker, its bright tones filling the space. "So once we can get these two off the stage, we're going to get ready for some dancing. So go pick your costumes. Dex and Maura, you lead the way and show them how it's done."

The man patted Dex on the shoulder and waved them away.

Great. She hadn't really expected to wear anything other than what she had on.

"Are you going over there?" she asked Dex as he went down the steps.

"Well, unless you want to be a—you know—party pooper."

He infused the words with a hint of challenge. One she was going to accept. "Party pooper? Oh, believe me, I can party with the best of them. I think I proved that at the bar."

Her heart took off, feeling lighter than it had in ages. And it was all because of Dex.

"So you did." He glanced at the racks of clothes and the curtains that cordoned off the dressing area behind it. "Okay, give me fifteen minutes and I'll meet you back out here."

More of the residents were joining them, sorting through the offerings and holding them up for each other to see. The sound of giggles and laughter were all around her.

Maura found a beige cowboy hat and tried it on for size and found a matching neckerchief. Well, that did it for her. She wasn't planning on doing a ton of dancing, so she would leave the rest of the clothes for the residents. It was their party, after all.

She moved over to the food and popped a strawberry into her mouth, glancing back over at the costume area. Dex still hadn't come out. Adjusting the hat on her head and feeling a little ridiculous, she ate another strawberry. She was hungry. Her stomach had been in knots all day at the thought of seeing him tonight and her appetite had fled for most of the day.

But it wasn't as awkward as she'd feared. In fact, Dex had seemed almost like a different person. So her belly was now sorting through the sights and scents of the food and trying to decide what she wanted to try first.

Just then Dex came out, and she stopped chewing and stared. He still had on his black jeans, but he'd exchanged his black shirt for a different one. This one, while still black, had a black-and-white floral yoke with the same detailing on the cuffs. Man, if anyone could pull that ensemble off, this man could—and did. His black cowboy hat gave him a bit of a bad-boy look and the black belt with its wide silver buckle made him look the epitome of a rodeo star.

He was gorgeous. Breathtaking. And she realized her jaws had locked themselves in place.

Chew, Maura, chew. The last thing she needed to do was choke on a strawberry.

She made her way over to him and circled him as if examining his outfit. She was, but she was also checking out the entire package.

"How'd I do?" he asked.

"I'd say you make a pretty passable cowboy. That shirt fits you surprisingly well." She reached up and adjusted the shoulders, not because they were crooked, but because she needed an excuse to touch him.

"So does yours."

She smiled. "That's because it's mine."

"I know."

The weirdness that had been between them after they'd left the bar—and after her subsequent revelation—seemed to be gone, but she couldn't help but address it. "Listen, I'm sorry about what happened. I shouldn't have said anything about the pregnancy."

"Yes, you should have. It just took me by surprise."

"I know, and I never meant you to learn about it like that."

"It's over and done, so let's just enjoy the night."

Before she went and ruined it? She hoped that wasn't what he was saying. But there was nothing in his face to indicate he was mad or upset. She was going to do as he suggested and try to have a good time.

He fingered the brim of her hat. "Nice touch."

"Ha! You look pretty at home in yours."

"Hmm... I've never owned a cowboy hat in my life."

Her head tilted. "You should. Your patients would probably have remarkable recoveries."

"Yeah...no. I'm not much of a rancher."

Honestly, Dex would probably look at home in almost any outfit he wore. Surfer dude? Check. Fisherman? Check. Surgeon? Already checked that box a couple of times.

"Well, you are now. For one night, anyway."

The caller was telling everyone who wasn't dancing to please clear the floor. "Dex and Maura? I'm going to need your assistance one more time, please."

Oh, no. What now?

She joined Dex on the dance floor. He gave her a look as if asking her what was going on. She didn't have a clue.

"I know a lot of you said you'd never square-danced before. Dex and Maura, have you done any?"

They both answered that they hadn't.

The caller smiled. "Well, that's perfect, because I'm going to prove that anyone can do it. Dex, stand over here while Maura and I demonstrate." He waited for a second, then held out his hand for Maura. She took it, a little disappointed that it wasn't Dex, before she tossed that thought aside.

"Ready?" he asked.

"I guess we'll find out." She forced a smile.

He adjusted the hands-free microphone at

his ear. "I'm going to go through four of the major dance moves and then I'm going to let Dex take over."

Her heart began to pound and she wasn't sure why. Hadn't she just wished he'd been her partner? Yes, but that was only when she'd thought there was no chance of that happening.

"Okay…do-si-do is done like this." Holding hands with her, he then asked her to face him as they both circled each other and came back to their original positions. "Let's try it again."

They repeated the move. Okay, that wasn't so hard. But when she glanced over at Dex, she saw he was standing to the side, arms crossed, a forbidding line between his brows. Because of the dance itself? Or because he was going to have to be paired up with her in a minute?

She realized she'd missed something the caller had said. "Sorry?"

"Things are going to be moving fast, once we really get going."

Was it her imagination or had he sent a sly smile Dex's way? Had he noticed how unhappy the surgeon was, as well? If so, he didn't seem to care.

They went through three other moves before calling a halt. "See there? You survived just fine, Maura. Now let's see what happens once we get Dex in here."

"I don't think—" Dex started, only to have the other man interrupt him.

"You'll have to try it sometime. Might as well show these ladies how it's done."

He came up beside her, seeming none too happy about being made to dance with her. "Sorry," she whispered.

Glancing at her, his expression softened. "It's okay."

"At least I'm not wearing a turquoise dress tonight," she said, playing on their earlier conversation.

"No, you're not."

The caller cleared his throat. "Let's start with do-si-do."

Instead of circling, though, they both stepped to the same side by mistake, only stopping when they were face-to-face. And far too close for comfort.

Her heart pounded all over again. "Looks like you don't need the dress."

She laughed. "You went the wrong way, not me."

A voice came over the loudspeaker. "If you two lovebirds are done chirping sweet nothings at each other, some of these ladies might want to dance tonight."

Laughter sounded from around the room, and Maura's face flamed to life. She could only imagine how it sounded with Dex saying she didn't need a dress.

"Let's try do-si-do again."

This time they managed to circle each other without incident, Dex sending her a slow smile as he stopped in front of her once again. This time on purpose.

"Very good." The caller smiled. "Now, Dex, hold her hands…"

Maura heard nothing beyond that because, when Dex did as the man asked, they ended up standing looking at each other, their hands clasped.

If their lives had been different, they might have stood just like this in front of a minister. As it was, they were standing in front of a paid event planner and this was all pretend.

Pretend. Just like she'd said to Dex after they'd made love.

Thankfully, the caller soon had them moving again, doing something different; otherwise, there was every chance Dex might have noticed something in her eyes. Something she really didn't want him to see.

But even though they were running through dance steps, she was very, very aware of him. Everything about him. His scent. The touch of his fingertips against hers. The reassuring squeeze of his hand when she almost ran into him once again.

"Okay, you guys, thanks for showing us that maybe not everyone is cut out for square dancing." He laughed, as did the residents. "But, seriously, you guys can see how easy it is. And we'll stick to these moves. For now. I'm sure Dex and Maura won't mind showing us some more steps once we've gotten these down." He gave them a wink that held far too much meaning. Did he think they were together?

Great. It wasn't like she could set him

straight in front of everyone. Nor did she need to. It wasn't like they were ever going to see him again after tonight.

The caller told everyone to grab a partner and get ready to have fun. "We have room for two squares, each one with four couples. Let's see what you've got. We'll take it easy on you. For now."

Women paired up with each other and with kids. Maura started to leave the floor only to be called back.

"We need one more couple in the second square."

Under her breath she muttered, "Oh, Lord."

"Surely dancing with me wasn't that repugnant." There was a stiffness to the words that made her glance up at him. "You didn't seem to mind dancing with him." He nodded in the caller's direction.

It wasn't repugnant at all. That was the problem. "He knew what he was doing."

The frown was back as he reached for her hand and tugged her toward him until they were in position. "I told you, I know nothing about square dancing."

"That's fine, that's fine," said the caller, obviously overhearing Dex's comment. "We're going to do the same steps we just went over. Has anyone here done any square dancing?"

Someone in their group raised her hand, and a couple of others did, as well.

"That's great. Okay, so your job is to help keep the rest of us straight."

She liked the way the man included himself in that. He was warm and encouraging, and knew how to instruct without being overbearing. Although Dex didn't seem to have warmed to him as much.

The music started and there was no more time to think as the caller started in with a singsong voice that reminded her of an auctioneer.

"Circle to the left and when you get home, do-si-do your own…"

Maura struggled to keep up with the calls. It was one thing to go through them slowly, one at a time. Putting the steps to music with one move following the other at a dizzying pace was a completely different story.

She careened hard into Dex. They stood staring at each other for a second before his face suddenly cleared and he laughed. He simply took her hand and promenaded like they were supposed to be doing.

She continued to struggle while Dex seemed to catch on with a grace and ease that reminded her of the Dex of old times. And she had to admit that he still had the power to make her breathless, just like he'd had when they were together.

She relaxed, finally letting herself enjoy what was happening. There was a lot of laughter, and no one was getting the moves perfect. Periodically, the caller would reset the squares so they could clear their heads and start all over. But every time Dex took her hands to promenade, a little butterfly whisked around her belly in time with the music. Those wings began to beat faster and faster until she was worried someone was going to figure out that she was enjoying this a little too much.

Thirty minutes later, the squares were supposed to form again to let those who hadn't gotten to dance a chance to join in. She took that as her chance to slide out of there.

Dex was stuck, however, since they needed

one more person. She stood on the sidelines and watched him dance.

His long legs carried him around the square, and he smiled at whoever he was partnered with, the corners of his eyes crinkling in a way that made her catch her breath.

A way that terrified her and made her realize she was letting him slide past her defenses all over again.

Don't go down this path. It didn't work the first time. It won't end any better a second time.

Did she really believe that?

How could she not? And even if she didn't, the man hadn't contacted her once over the last week other than to type those impersonal messages about the party.

Which from what she could see was a wild success. She glanced over at the bull, which was going in a very slow circle. One of the moms was sitting on it along with her young child whose smile lit up her insides, making her forget about what she should and shouldn't be feeling today.

It was okay to just stop and enjoy herself. She could worry about the rest tomorrow.

The second dance ended, and Dex came out to join her, lifting his hat and running his hand over his hair, before settling it back in place. He reminded her of a country and western crooner who sang of heartbreak and hope. Of sunshine and pain. All she wanted today, though, was the sunshine, with none of the pain.

"That was harder than it looked," he said.

"You made it look easy, actually. Sorry for crashing into you that one time."

He grinned. "You can crash into me any time you'd like, even without the prom dress."

Yep. Sunshine. Not a cloud in sight. At least not right now.

He said something else that she missed entirely. "Sorry. What?"

"I asked what time the gifts are going to be handed out?"

"Around seven or so." She glanced at her watch and saw it was six thirty. The time was flying by far too quickly.

There were people sitting on the straw bales eating. She'd forgotten she was hungry. "Do you want to grab a bite to eat?"

"That sounds good."

They loaded up a couple of plates and found a spot to sit. Dex set his cup down next to him on the straw. "I'd say this was a success, wouldn't you?"

"Yes. I'm glad to see Sylvia out there." She spotted the woman across the way, sending her a wave. She was gratified to see her smile. "And I'm really glad the square dance leader said what he did. I had no idea."

"About his daughter?"

"Yes. I think it gives them hope that life isn't over just because someone abused their trust and hurt them. They can still be happy. With or without a partner."

"It certainly gave them something to think about."

Did he disagree with the man? Surely Dex had had his share of happiness over the years. Although her marriage had failed, it hadn't completely soured her on the idea that she could still find joy in the things of life.

"It's better than being paralyzed and stuck in the same place year after year, don't you think?"

He shot her a look, but didn't answer.

Did he think that's what she was? Paralyzed and stuck? She'd admit that after her divorce she had been for a while. But now that she'd made some decisions about her future, she was finally ready to move forward again.

Dex scraped at a piece of pasta on his plate. "I think everyone has their own timetable. It's not always as cut-and-dried as people like to think."

Okay, so it didn't sound like he'd been thinking about her, after all. Maybe it was a generalized statement.

Or maybe it was about him. She remembered his white-knuckled grip on the steering wheel when it had started snowing.

Maybe he thought she was judging him. "Hey, I wasn't talking about you. I was referring to the women here. I took what the guy said as a message of hope and encouragement. I think it took a lot of courage for him to share about his daughter. It made me glad we chose that particular company."

"You may not have been talking about me, but it hit home. About me. About my mom. She's never gotten over the accident. She's been under the care of a psychiatrist for years. And I—"

Sylvia and her son came over and interrupted whatever he'd been about to say. "Weston is asking for you to try Bully."

"Bully?" Dex asked.

"The bull."

"Ah… I don't—"

Maura spoke up. "You saw how slow it was going earlier. I'm sure they'll take it easy on you. Besides it knocked something loose in me, remember? Maybe it'll do the same for you."

"It knocked you off balance, if I remember right." Sending her a look that promised revenge, he got to his feet and handed her his plate. "Save that for me, would you? Hopefully, I'll be well enough to eat it when I come back."

Sylvia laughed, her smile big and beautiful. "See, Wes? Dr. Chamblisse is going to try it."

She watched Dex walk away with the mother and son, his back ramrod straight, his steps sure and steady.

His voice said one thing, but his movements said another. This was one man who didn't show fear.

Except when it snowed.

That didn't make him weak in her eyes. It made him real and like every other human being on the planet, affected by the things that life tossed at you.

He was the sexiest man she'd ever known. And she doubted that would ever change. She might have moved on, but it didn't mean Dex had magically changed. It meant she had. Just like back then, she wasn't willing to settle for a man who held back the most important things in his life. Like trust. And sharing of burdens.

And love.

He got on the bull and held on, glancing over at her just before the operator turned the machine on. It started off in a circle, slow with up-and-down ripples of movement. Dex had no trouble staying on. Weston stood on the outside of the protective tubes and jumped up and down. She could have sworn she heard the boy yell, "Bully!"

Two minutes went by and then three, the bull getting a little more energetic with each pass, but nothing as crazy as the one at the bar. And then the ride slowed and came to a stop. He'd managed to stay on the entire time.

After getting off, he bent down to say something to Weston, and her throat grew tight. Two weeks ago, he had said that she would make a great mother. Well, he would have made a wonderful dad, despite his past.

Committing to a person because you wanted to spend the rest of your life with them was one thing. Dex hadn't been willing to do that. But having a child, and the blood connection that brought, was another thing. She was pretty sure Dex would have taken on that challenge even when he'd been unwilling—or unable—to promise her any kind of forever.

But maybe forever was overrated. Look at her and Gabe. They'd stood before a minister and promised to stay together come what may. That promise had been broken. So why make it at all?

Maybe taking things one day at a time— one night at a time—was a better way. Kind of like what they did the night they slept together. If they hadn't both made it weird, maybe it wouldn't have been.

Dex made his way back to her, and she

handed him back his plate. "See? You didn't fall off at all."

"I couldn't let the little guy down."

"And you didn't. He looked pretty happy from where I'm sitting."

A slight frown marred his brow. "You're looking mighty pleased with yourself about something."

"I've just been thinking about how complicated people make life, when maybe it doesn't need to be that way. When maybe we're just meant to grab whatever happiness we can and hold on for as long as it lasts. Until life grows too frenetic, like that bull. And when that happens, we simply let go and fall away. No regrets. No saying we didn't enjoy the ride."

"This coming from the girl who'd once needed relationships to last forever."

"At the time, that's what I thought was important. I think I'm changing my mind." She caught his eyes. "Maybe one night is all I need, Dex."

His brows went up. "One night?"

"Yes. One night."

CHAPTER NINE

HE WAS ALMOST certain Maura had issued an invitation.

One he wasn't about to turn down, since he'd been thinking along the same lines for the last two weeks. Which was why he'd avoided calling her. Hearing her voice would have made it impossible not to ask to see her.

And he knew what would happen if he did.

Sitting through that gift exchange at the end of the party had seemed to take forever, and they hadn't been able to leave because Maura was in charge of handing out the presents. Weston's face, when he saw his giraffe, had been priceless. Good thing it was a toy, because if the child had squeezed a real giraffe that way, he was pretty sure the animal would have passed out from lack of oxygen.

But then it was over. And as they pulled out

of the parking lot just after nine o'clock, he still wasn't certain where things stood with them. Until she put a hand on his thigh.

Okay, the invitation hadn't been in his imagination. It had been very, very real.

They'd both agreed the last time had been a mistake. So what had changed her mind?

Hell, did it even matter?

His body was telling him it definitely did not. He would take what he could get. And, like she said, they could just walk away at any time. Although the word she'd used had been "fall," which didn't sound nearly as easy.

But holding on could be even harder when things got too crazy. A little whisper went through his head that he brushed away. Of course he would choose to let go of the rope and hobble away. It's what Dex did. It's what he knew.

"We're going back to my place."

"Fine." She threw the word out with a nonchalance that wasn't like her, but it didn't make him change direction and take her home.

Could he really settle for one night?

Definitely. Because it was better than no nights at all.

They made it to his two-story home on the outskirts of the city. The house was bigger than he needed since it was just him, but he'd gotten the place for a steal. An elderly couple had wanted to downsize just as Dex was starting to look for something more permanent than a rental house. He'd snapped it up and had lived here for the last five years.

Unlike Maura's whites and creams, his place was all about dark wood and heavy, immovable furniture. Maybe because that's what his life had felt like. Or maybe it was like Maura had said: he was paralyzed and unable to move on. The big weighty pieces kept him anchored in place figuratively and literally.

Maura's hand was still on his thigh. Picking it up, he carried her palm to his mouth and pressed his lips against it. The smile she gave him clogged his senses. He wasn't positive this was really happening. But she sure looked real. Felt real.

They were back in their regular clothes, having left the cowboy hats and the "yee-haws" with the owner of Square Dancers R Us. They were no longer in the pretend world of the party.

He didn't want her to be disappointed by what she found inside. Or didn't find. "I don't have any Christmas decorations up."

It was two days before Christmas, and it seemed kind of a shame to let the date go by unnoticed, but wasn't this a much better present than a tree or lights?

It was for him. He wasn't sure about her.

"I don't care about the decorations, Dex. I'll be unwrapping the only present I want to see in just a few minutes. You." She leaned over and toyed with the skin where his shirt collar opened.

He swallowed. How was it that this woman knew exactly what to say to turn him inside out? Made him want her more than any other woman alive?

Sliding his hand in her hair, he tugged her close enough to kiss her. And the second his lips met hers, he was lost. So much for reality. She turned his world into a dream that he never wanted to wake up from, never wanted to leave.

"Inside. Now."

She laughed, but it was a little shaky. "I agree. But what kind of inside are we talking about? Inside? Or…*inside*."

He leaned forward and kissed her again. "Do I actually have to choose one or the other?"

"No. I just wanted to see which you wanted first."

With that, he snapped the door open and got out. "Don't tempt me. I'm pretty sure the neighbor to my left has a camera on his property. I don't think you want to be an internet sensation."

"Yikes! Probably not."

He opened her door and held his hand out. When she accepted it, he squeezed his fingers around it. He'd always loved holding her hand. Loved the way it felt to tow her behind him and know for sure that she was right there.

He hadn't realized how much he'd missed it until just this minute.

Or maybe he had. But he'd known there was no hope. Especially once he'd heard about her marriage.

He got her through the front door and slammed it behind her. Pressed her back against it. "There. Now, we're inside."

"Not quite. But you will be."

His chuckle came from a molten place within him. He moved close, pressing against her, his hands on either side of her head. "You're killing me here, Maura. I want this to last. Want you here all night."

"Don't you have someplace to be in the morning?"

"Mmm. I do. Yes." His hands slid to her butt and lifted her against him. Her legs wrapped around his hips as he carried her through the living room, past the kitchen and down the hallway to where his master suite was. After entering it, he bypassed his bed and went into the adjoining bathroom. He set her on the countertop, keeping his body between her legs, his swollen flesh already tight behind his zipper.

When her fingers went to her blouse, he shook his head. "No. My turn."

He made quick work of unbuttoning her white shirt, guiding it down her arms but leaving it over her wrists. Her white lacy bra pushed her breasts up, the soft skin beckoning to him.

He leaned over and kissed one of the soft mounds, his lips sliding up her neck.

Her breath hissed as he nipped the sensitive area just below her ear.

Then he found the snap on her jeans and undid it, slowly easing her zipper down. "Lift up."

She did as he asked and he tugged the garment off, letting it fall to the floor along with her black pumps.

Sitting on his counter in his bathroom, in just her bra and matching panties, she looked like a goddess. All feminine and sweet, yet with a raw edge of sexiness that drove him to madness. "You are gorgeous."

He reached behind her and raked his fingers through her hair, loving the way it was like silk across her skin. She was irresistible.

And tonight he wasn't even going to try.

He quickly divested himself of his clothes and sheathed himself before moving back to her, kissing her deeply.

His fingers slipped beneath the elastic on her panties and dipped lower, until he found what he was looking for. She was warm and wet, and that satiny skin would feel like heaven around him.

Maura moaned, her head tipping back, eyes fluttering shut as she gave herself over to what he was doing. He'd said he wanted it to last, but he was no longer sure he would be able to fulfill that promise as his body was demanding more and more and cursing when he offered it nothing.

Keeping one hand where it was, he used his other to pull her to the very edge of the counter.

"Oh, Dex…"

Hell. The way she said his name…

He made his strokes firmer, her hips beginning to move in time with each touch, lifting and falling in a way that mimicked what he wanted. What he needed.

And the sounds she made. Low. Throaty.

He was home. Back beside the creek. Making love in the shallows as the water gurgled around their bodies.

Sliding two fingers inside, he crooked them, continuing to stroke her with his thumb as he added slight pressure to the spot he knew she liked. He needed her to come. Wanted to know he still had the power to make her as mad for him as he was for her.

Come on, baby. Give it to me.

He quickened his pace, nipping at her lips, her jawline, her neck, before leaning back to watch her.

Her lips parted and she grabbed several quick breaths, hips lifting...reaching...

Her eyes flashed open and focused on him for a split second before she yanked her hands from the sleeves of her shirt and grabbed his shoulders.

He pulled aside the crotch of her panties and plunged home. She wrapped her legs around him the way she had when he'd carried her in here as he rode her, her movements every bit as sinuous as they'd been when she was riding that bull the night at the bar. Watching her had been a turn-on then, but it was nothing compared to having her here in his arms, acting like she couldn't get enough of him.

It was the same for him. He couldn't get enough of this women. Never had, never would, no matter how many times they had sex together.

It was earthy and raw and exactly the way he liked it. The way he liked her.

He thrust harder even as she nibbled at his lips, whispering against them. And when he could hold back no longer, he entered deep and went rigid as he spasmed, pouring everything he had into her.

When it was over, his legs went weak. Mind numbed to everything except the memory of what had just happened.

Keeping the connection for as long as possible, he carried her back into the bedroom and laid her gently on the bed, shuddering as he slid free.

Her hair was wild and free across his pillow. His side of the bed.

Accident? Or had he meant to put her there?

Right now he didn't know. There were too many tangled emotions trying to surface. He just kept pushing them back under. He didn't want to think. Didn't want to do anything except lie beside her and relish the feel of her next to him.

Except he wanted her naked. Completely naked.

He leaned over and slid her undergarment down her legs and undid her bra. She yawned up at him, her beautiful face shining up at him. She looked just like the Maura from many years ago. The Maura he'd slept with... the Maura he'd loved.

"Tired?" he asked, running the tip of his finger down her nose.

"Mmm...no. Happy."

The words the square dance caller had used came back to him, sending a slow shiver down his spine. *That's what we all want, isn't it? The chance to be happy?*

She'd been happy with him once before. Until he'd destroyed everything by telling her he couldn't be what she needed him to be.

He couldn't be then...and he couldn't be now, if he were honest with himself.

Why? The question thumped in the background, getting louder and louder until it demanded an answer.

An answer he didn't have, except that he came with too much baggage, feared loss far too much to try to hold on to anything. Certainly not something as elusive as happiness.

Hell, he'd even lost a baby without knowing about it. What if she'd told him about the miscarriage back then?

Another thought struck him. What if she'd died during it? Or during childbirth?

He suddenly couldn't look at her without an abrupt sense of panic stabbing through him. His heart pounded, and his mouth went dry.

What if she'd died? Just like most of his family had.

He needed to get out of this room. Now.

Heading toward the door, he stopped when she called out to him. "Where are you going?"

She was half-sitting up in bed, a strange expression on her face.

He cast around for something to say and grabbed the first thing that came to mind. "Just to bring us something to drink. I'll be right back."

The tension in her face eased, and she lay back down, not bothering to cover her breasts. "Okay, then. Don't be long."

"I won't."

He moved through the doorway, stopping

just outside the room to lean a shoulder against the wall. What the hell was wrong with him?

Why were these old feelings slamming into him again? The fear he'd had all those years ago that Maura would die, too, and he'd be left totally alone.

He'd had sex with women since he and Maura had ended things. But he couldn't remember feeling this unsettled—this *afraid*—with any of them. He'd had the same sensation two weeks ago, before finally deciding he'd imagined it.

It was obvious he hadn't. Because right now the sweaty palms, the jittery sense of doom, was all very real. It was the exact same sensation he got when…

When it snowed.

When there were reports of black ice.

When he heard the sound of an ambulance screaming its way down the highway.

His hands fisted against his sides, another wave of horror washing through him and threatening to bring him to his knees. His eyes burned as a wall of water built up behind them.

God. Not now. Not when she might come out and see him.

Forcing himself to move, he tried to power his way through the maze his mind had constructed. But it was hopeless. He was lost. Just as he'd been for the last fifteen years.

He went into the kitchen and got two glasses for water. He put a couple of ice cubes in each one before stopping and studying the contents of the cabinet.

To hell with water. He needed something else. Getting down a third glass, he moved over to the bar. Picking up a bottle, he poured a finger of whiskey into the tumbler and bolted the contents down in one swift motion. The liquid seared his esophagus and hit his stomach with a jolt, the warmth spreading throughout his body. The only place it didn't touch was the iciness of his heart. But at least his mouth wasn't as parched.

It was the only thing that wasn't.

He planted his hand on the bar, holding himself up as he sloshed another measure into the tumbler. He squeezed his eyes shut.

"Dammit. What the hell am I doing here?"

He opened his eyes and gazed into the

steady amber liquid as if it might have all the answers. But of course it didn't. He'd just put the rim to his lips when he stopped, his glance meeting Maura's. She was standing in the doorway, wrapped in a sheet, staring at him. Her expression was...stricken.

He'd seen that expression before. Had seen it in his dreams many times over the years.

It was the same expression she'd had fifteen years ago after she'd stood in front of him and asked him where he saw their relationship going. When he'd told her he didn't know.

He tipped the glass and swallowed the drink. Put the tumbler down.

She didn't say anything for a long minute before finally breaking the silence. "That bad, huh?"

"I don't know what you mean." The lie came out quickly. Easily.

She turned and nodded at the tall glasses on the counter. The ice in them was melting. "You said you were coming out to get us drinks. I just didn't realize you needed something a whole lot stronger than water to face coming back to the bedroom."

"It's not that."

"Really? Then why don't you tell me what it is."

He had no idea. He'd been standing here trying to figure it out, only to come up blank. "I really don't know."

"It's okay. I think I do." She licked her lips and drew the sheet tighter. She probably didn't realize it, but her silhouette was highlighted by the light in the hallway, every slender curve visible to him. He wanted it. He wanted it all. Wanted the happiness that old square dancer had talked about.

But dammit, he couldn't have it. Because the stuff sloshing behind his need of her was corrosive, eating away at his gut and leaving him a hollowed-out shell. The same shell that had been left after the accident.

He didn't deserve to be happy, no matter what anyone said.

His brain knew that wasn't true. But his emotions? They sabotaged him each time he reached out to grasp at it.

To grasp at her.

She tossed her hair behind her shoulder. "I'm going to go, Dex. I've already called a cab. This was a mistake. Somehow I always knew it was, but I'd… It doesn't matter. You won't have to worry about it anymore. Or about me." Tears shimmered in her eyes, and she swiped at them with an angry stroke of her hand. "I hope someday you find what you need. I only hope it isn't too late when you do."

With that, she turned on her heel and disappeared down the hallway. To get dressed probably.

He made no move to follow her.

Because he'd already found what he needed. Except, she was right. It was too late. At least for him. He poured another drink, moved into his living room and sat on his sofa. This time he didn't gulp it. He sipped it, biding his time as he listened to every sound she made back in his bedroom.

He should go to her. Talk to her. Take her back to bed and make everything okay.

But he didn't, because there was no way anything would ever be okay. He'd only be delaying the inevitable. Or, worse, hurt her all over again.

So he sat there as he heard her pull his bedroom door shut with a soft click. As the sound of her footsteps came down his hallway. As she edged past the back of the sofa where he sat. As the front door opened and then closed.

And then she was gone.

Dex shut his eyes and leaned his head against the back of the sofa. Some men might have considered this a win—evading the cuddles and pillow talk that came after getting what they wanted.

But it wasn't a win. He would never see this as anything other than a big fat loss. A loss of what could have been. Of what had been. A loss he would never get over be it fifteen years or seventy years.

And Dex had no idea how to make it anything other than what it was.

CHAPTER TEN

It was Christmas.

But it sure didn't feel like it.

Maura hadn't heard from Dex since she'd left the house two days ago. Then again, she hadn't tried to call him either. And she wouldn't. She was really and truly done. When she'd seen him chug that drink like it was water and then pour himself another, she knew. He was having a panic attack. One that being with her had caused. And that just about killed her.

It would just happen again and again, and she was not willing to cause him even more pain and suffering than she already had.

To stay and watch him go through it had been too hard, so she'd let go and fallen away. Just like she'd told Dex she would.

She'd decided to take some personal time,

which she'd saved up over the last couple of years, to try to decide what to do from here. The first thing she was going to do, though, was some award-winning pretending—something she'd suggested Dex do after they'd slept together that first time. She was going to act like it was Christmas and pretend it was a time of celebration.

She was going to do for herself what she'd helped do for the women at the center with that party the hospital had thrown: keep herself so busy that she had no time to stop and think about how much pain she was in.

Because it was deep. And seemed endless. And she was pretty sure she wasn't strong enough to climb out of the pit she found herself in. At least not today.

She would, though, just like she'd done once before.

So she'd gone to the big-box store in the center of town, where a few straggly trees sat looking almost as lonely as she was. She'd been half-surprised the store was open today, and she was glad it was. Because the more she moved, the less she thought.

She glanced at her car with its minuscule

roof, trying to decide if she could at least strap the smallest of the trees to the top of it. Surely that four-foot one over there would be okay. She went over and stood beside it before paying the clerk, who was shivering in temperatures that had suddenly dropped well below freezing.

"Sorry about this," she said. "I just didn't plan things very well."

Ha! She hadn't planned them at all. And she certainly hadn't planned what had happened with Dex.

"It's okay. I have to be out here anyway. At least for another hour." He put the tree through a machine that bound the branches to the trunk and encased it in some kind of netting. Then he helped her set it on top of her car and ratcheted it tight with the straps she'd brought.

At least she'd planned for that. She wasn't entirely hopeless.

"Thanks." She waved to him and tossed the bag of lights and ornaments she'd bought to go on the tree into the car. She got in, giving an exasperated laugh when she saw the tree trunk hanging over the front of her car.

The chuckle faded when the memory of Dex all scrunched up in her passenger seat came back to her. He'd almost been too big for her car. Just like the tree that now sat on top of it.

It was okay. She'd just go slow.

Like she'd done with Dex?

She rolled her eyes and pulled out of the lot, creeping along as the wind tugged at her vehicle. The streets were pretty much deserted, thank God. Everyone else was smart. They were all in their nice warm homes, celebrating with their families.

Well, Maura had already gone to her folks' house and tried to smile her way through brunch, exchanging the presents they'd gotten one another. She was glad she'd been able to get out of there before her mom sensed something was wrong and asked her about it. They'd had no idea that Dex had wandered back into her life, if only for a short time. Or that he was right back out of it again.

This time it was for good. She would make sure of that. When a sharp gust pulled at the vehicle, it wobbled a bit before righting itself. The tree had made the car a little more top-heavy than normal. Maybe getting it had been a bad idea.

No. This was step one of getting back to normal. She was going to celebrate Christmas, dammit, if it killed her.

She rounded a sharp downhill corner in the road, easing off the gas as she did. If she remembered right, there was a stoplight just ahead.

There. She saw it.

Her peripheral vision caught sight of something shimmering on the black asphalt in front of her. She looked and realized too late that it was a patch of ice that had developed from the rain earlier today.

The light. Oh, God. It was red!

Her muscles went rigid, and she tried to tap her brakes, but the momentum of the corner and the downhill slope sent her car into a sideways skid that picked up speed as she went. It dragged her right through the red light, barely missing another car as she struggled to regain control of the car. It was no use. She was going to crash. A light post loomed on her left and she hit it with enough force to slam her head against the driver's side window. Stunned, she sat there for a minute or two, her vision spinning around and around. She blinked, trying to clear it. She lifted a hand to feel for blood and winced as a sharp pain went through her wrist.

The world still slowly spun, and about every third rotation she spotted the tree trunk of her Christmas tree, lying in the exact spot it had been strapped.

Well, at least something had come through unscathed. In the distance she heard the eerie sound of her car horn blaring. She put her uninjured hand to her ear and tried to do the shake that had cleared those damned crystals last time, but it didn't work. Okay, she needed to at least call for help. Except her phone was nowhere to be seen.

She really hadn't meant the whole thing about celebrating Christmas if it killed her.

She needed to get out of the car.

Just then the passenger's side door opened and a woman peered in at her. "Are you okay? You slid past me through the intersection."

"Was that you?" Her thoughts were fuzzy and it took a lot of effort to continue. "Can you help me get out?"

"I called 911. They told me not to move you."

"Oh, that's right." She was a doctor. She should know that. "Okay. Is—is my tree okay?"

The woman cocked her head and looked at her like she was crazy. "Your tree is fine. You should be more worried about you."

"I'm okay. Just a bump on the head and a sprained wrist." Except her wrist was hurting more and more. Maybe she'd broken it. Great. That was all she needed. How was she going to string lights with a broken wrist?

She took a deep breath as an urge to laugh appeared out of nowhere. Maybe the woman was right. Why was she worried about a tree?

The wail of a siren, joined by another one, sounded off in the distance. "At least the door opened."

"I'm sorry?"

"I won't need the jaws of life." This time the laughter couldn't be contained, though it sounded weird. Like it was coming from someone else. Okay, maybe she had a concussion in addition to her bum wrist.

Another head poked in the door next to

the woman. She recognized him—he was a paramedic from the hospital. The laughter dried up.

"Ugh. I'm sorry you had to come out on Christmas night for my little fender bender. Why are you on that side of the car?"

"Have you seen the door on your side?"

"No. Is it bad?"

"Yep. We're going to have to get you out this side. Are you injured?"

"I sprained my wrist."

She heard the woman behind her. "She's been kind of out of it, talking about the Jaws of Life and worried about her Christmas tree. And I saw her rub her head."

She heard him speaking in hushed tones to someone else asking them to call ahead to the hospital. Then he popped his head back in. "You probably know the routine. We're going to stabilize your head and neck and slide you out of the car."

"Are you kidding me? I can scoot over if you'll help me."

"Do I look like I'm kidding?" The man's face was stern, without even a hint of humor.

"I guess not."

Five minutes later they had a backboard and neck brace in place, but when they went to slide her free of the car, someone's hand pressed on her left side and a moan slid out before she could stop it.

"What?"

"I—I just have a little something going on with my side." This was ridiculous. She'd been driving at practically a snail's pace. "I was going slow because of the tree. I shouldn't be hurt at all."

He looked her in the eye. "That tree probably saved your life. The salt trucks are doing their best, but the roads are icing up fast, and they're forecasting an inch or two of snow tonight."

Snow. Dex hated the snow. She remembered his white-knuckle grip on the steering wheel, and suddenly she was crying without really knowing why.

She was still crying when they got her out and lifted her onto the stretcher.

She tried to wave him off, giving a soggy hiccup as she did. "Can someone just run me home? I'm okay. Really." She was horrified that she might break down completely and that someone might guess the reason. Or, worse, that she might see Dex at the hospital and he might ask why she was so distraught over a tiny little accident.

It was normal to be upset, right? No matter how inconsequential her injuries.

Except this was how his dad and sisters had died. She didn't want to see his face when it all came back to him. It would be the same face he'd had as he threw back drink after drink at his house.

It was the same face that had caused her to walk out all over again.

"Sorry, no can do. Your hand is already swelling, and you've got some pain in your left quadrant, which means you probably have a broken rib or two from the side impact."

She was suddenly too tired to argue. "Okay, if you really think it's necessary, I'll go. What about my car?"

"I have your purse and your keys. It'll have to be towed."

So much for putting up a tree. Looked like she wouldn't even get to do that. She bit back another spurt of emotion. She must have a concussion. She was never this weepy.

Even after leaving Dex's house, she hadn't sobbed. Maybe this was all part of the grief process.

They arrived at the hospital fifteen minutes later. Maura's world had finally stopped spinning in circles, although her head still hurt. They ran her through the ER, and she found herself having to refrain from issuing orders or pronouncing her own diagnosis to the attending physician.

It was weird being the one lying on the gurney rather than standing over it. A thought came to her, and she grabbed the hand of one of the nurses. "Dr. Chamblisse isn't here, is he?"

The woman blinked at her, but if she thought the question odd, she didn't react. "I think I saw him leave about thirty minutes ago. Do you want me to call him?"

"No! I mean no. We just had a patient in common and I wanted to…"

She wanted to what? Discuss it. There was no way the nurse would buy that. She glued her lips together so she couldn't say anything else stupid.

At least that meant she wouldn't be running

into him. It was exactly why she'd decided to take some time off. To figure out if she could even face seeing him day in and day out. If her fear of him being at the hospital was any indicator, the answer to that was no.

She had no idea what she was going to do if that was the case.

"We're going to run you up to X-Ray and see what's going on with that hand and wrist—your ribs, too. I also think you have a mild concussion."

Maura leaned back against the pillow. "I see why he hates winter so much."

"Sorry?"

"Nothing. Just talking to myself."

While she was waiting for her turn in Radiology, a nurse came with a pill and a cup of water. "The doctor thought you might appreciate a little something to take the edge off."

She was right. The pain had been steadily building, especially when she moved her left side. She swallowed the meds down. "Thanks. I'm sure I'll be better by tomorrow."

Really? Was she sure about that? Now that she'd had time to think, the clawing pain that had assailed her ever since she'd left Dex's house was back. She'd been able to ignore it over the last two days by filling her time up to the max, buying presents for her family, catching up on housework and a bunch of other trivial stuff. But now that she was lying on a gurney with nothing to do but think, the pain was back. And it was the kind of ache that no amount of medicine would take away.

They were finally ready for her, and although it hurt to slide from the gurney onto the X-ray table, the pill the nurse had given her was starting to kick in. They were done with her pretty quickly and she glanced at the tech. "See anything?"

He gave her a knowing smile. "I'll let the doc get with you about that."

"I'll bet you say that to all your patients."

His smile widened. "All the ones who dare to ask."

She came out of X-Ray, and they put her in a room down the hall. Surely they weren't keeping her overnight.

Except how would she even get home? She had no car.

The thought of lying in the hospital with nothing to do but dwell on what had happened at Dex's house terrified her. Because as he'd gotten up to go into the kitchen, she realized that she still loved him. Which meant that all her flippant remarks about only wanting sex from him were a smoke screen, an attempt to hide the truth: that she desperately hoped she might be wrong about him. That he might still care for her. Might be able to finally commit to being with her forever.

Then she'd caught him chugging down liquor like he couldn't erase the image of her fast enough.

God, how could she have been so very stupid. She wasn't a kid anymore. She was a grown-up who should be better able to make rational decisions.

Smart decisions. Decisions that wouldn't—

A knock sounded at her door.

Maybe that was the doctor with her X-ray results. Maybe she wouldn't have to stay after all.

The person who opened that door was definitely not that doctor.

She swallowed hard. It was Dex.

This couldn't be happening.

Why? Why now?

Did he want to grind home the fact that there was no hope? That what was once over and done was still over and done?

Well, there was no need. He'd gotten that across loud and clear. "I thought you'd left for the night."

"I did. I just got off the phone with my mom, actually. We had a long overdue talk about moving on and living life." His face was deadly serious. "And then I heard you'd been in an accident. I came back."

He came back because she crashed.

Only because she'd crashed.

Her heart crumbled into ashes. That was almost as bad as when she'd toyed with telling him about the pregnancy and how afraid she'd been that he would only want to be with her because of the baby.

Her voice came out a little harsher than she meant it to. "As you can see, I'm just fine. There was no need to change whatever plans you'd had for tonight. Especially not on Christmas. You should go see your mom."

"You misunderstood. I didn't change my plans because of the accident. I changed them because of you. I was actually headed to your house when the call came through."

"You were? Why? I thought you said you'd just gotten off the phone with your mother."

"I did. I called her. Because I can't get that man's words out of my head. It's why I was coming over to see you, next."

She had no idea what he was talking about. "What man?"

"The caller at the hoedown. He said, 'That's what we all want, isn't it? The chance to be happy.'"

She remembered him saying that. But she didn't see how it changed anything. "Sometimes it just doesn't work that way. As much as we might want to be happy, it just isn't in the cards. Let go of the bull and fall, remember?"

"But what if I don't want to fall this time? What if I want to hold on tight until the very end of the ride?"

The pain pills must be impairing her cognitive skills. "I don't understand."

"I sat down over the last two days and played back everything that was said when you came to my house. And although the words were different than the ones that ended our relationship fifteen years ago, the underlying issue was still there—fear. I threw it all away because I was afraid. Because I didn't think I deserved to be happy. My mom and my heart finally told me otherwise."

He took her uninjured hand in his, and her eyes prickled in dangerous ways. "I don't want to make the same mistake, Maura. This time, I want to hold on."

"And if you change your mind and break my heart all over again…?" Her words scraped past a rough patch in her throat and she ended in a whisper. "Please don't."

A muscle worked in his jaw. "Hell, Maura, I am so sorry. Sorry for what I put you through back then. And sorry for what I did at the house. I have no right to ask you for another chance…" He gave a visible swallow. "But here I am."

"You want a second chance? For what?"

"For us. Because I realized two nights ago that I was still in love with you, and it scared me shitless. Tonight, I finally worked through my fears and decided I could either let all the what-ifs destroy any chance for happiness.

Or I could change them and force those same what-ifs to look toward good things."

"Good things?"

He nodded. "Like what if I kick my fear in the teeth and ask you to marry me. Like what if I ask you to have those babies you talked about having earlier. Only they'd be *my* babies."

She stared at him. "I really do have a concussion."

"What?"

"If I'm imagining all this and wake up tomorrow alone in this bed, I am going to come and find you. And you won't like it when I do."

He kissed her hand. "You're not imagining it. And I probably deserve whatever bad things you want to do to me, because I've wanted to do them to myself for years. But I hope you'll believe me when I say I love you. I want to spend the rest of my life with you."

He took a shuddery breath. "When I heard you'd slid on some ice and hit a light pole, I was frantic. They were bringing you in and wouldn't tell me how you were. You can't imagine where my thoughts were."

"I think I can."

"The whole drive back to the hospital, my brain fixated on all the time I'd wasted worrying about what could happen. I'd rather be with you for whatever time we both have on this earth than do nothing and wake up wishing I'd done things differently. So what do you say?"

She tilted her head, only to have the world roll to one side. "Whoa, remind me not to do that again. And if you're serious about asking me to marry you, the answer to that is yes. I love you, too, Dex. And I want to spend whatever time I have left on this earth with you as well. And with those babies we're going to make. Six? Seven?"

When his eyes widened, she laughed. "I'm kidding. I'm fine with one or two."

"How do you know I didn't consider six or seven a lowball number?"

"Um, yeah...no."

"Okay, one or two it is."

She pulled her hand from his and reached up to touch his face. "I need you to do something for me."

"Okay, what is it?"

"I need you to find out where they took my car."

He smiled. "I'm pretty sure I'm going to call your parents first, so they know what happened to you."

"I'm serious." For some reason, it was suddenly very important that he find her car.

"Did you leave something in it?"

"No, I left something *on* it, and I really, really need it. Especially now."

He looked at her like she was crazy, and maybe she was.

"What is it?"

"It's my Christmas tree. The guy I bought it from at the store was shivering from the cold, and yet he still wrapped that tree for me and helped me strap it on top of the car." The tears that came to her eyes this time were ones of gratitude. "I drove really slowly because of that tree. The EMT says it probably saved my life."

"Thank God." He leaned down and pressed his cheek against hers. "I'll find the car, honey. And when I do, I'm taking that tree to my house and giving it the treatment it deserves. The treatment you deserve."

Her voice was shaky as she tried to find something humorous to say. Something that wouldn't turn her into a wet dishrag. "You're stealing my tree?"

"Not exactly. But when they finally spring you from this place, you're coming home with me. I'm not spending one more night without you by my side."

"It's for real, this time, isn't it?"

He didn't ask her what she was talking about. They both knew.

"Yes, Maura. It's for real." He kissed her softly on the mouth. "And this time, you'd better hold on. Because it's forever."

"Forever." The word came out as a sigh.

"All anyone wants is to be happy," he murmured against her mouth. "And that includes you. And me."

EPILOGUE

One year later

CHRISTMAS MUSIC FLOATED through the house as Dex threw more tinsel on the tree until the box was almost empty. "A little more on the left."

"If I put any more weight on that side of the tree it's going to topple over."

She threw him a fake glare. "Is that a euphemism for my belly?"

He left what he was doing and came over to her, kissing her forehead. "Your belly is gorgeous, Maura. Just like the rest of you."

"Good answer." She groaned. "But if little Noah doesn't come soon, I'm going to have to go through Lamaze classes all over again. It's been ages." The baby was a week overdue and seemed to be in no hurry to put in an appearance.

"The doctor said there's no reason to worry. Not yet."

She glanced out the window and saw the first flakes of snow. She tensed, glancing at her husband.

"I know. And I'm fine."

They'd talked through all his baggage regarding the snow and what had happened to his family. He had told her he now realized there was good and bad in everything. What had happened had been awful, no doubt about it. But it had also brought them together in the end. That slip on a patch of ice had knocked some sense into both of them.

He tossed the empty tinsel package into the kitchen garbage and then came over and sat beside her. He'd started a fire in the fireplace a few hours earlier and the sounds of crackling wood was heavenly.

She couldn't be happier. She had the man of her dreams, and soon they'd have a little one to share their lives with.

Sliding her fingers into those of her husband, she leaned her head against him with a sigh. "I love you so much, Dex."

"Right there with you, babe."

A twinge in her abdomen made her jump. "Speaking of babes…"

Dex glanced down. "Kicking again?"

"I'm not sure. I think… Oh!"

Her hand went to her stomach, rubbing in little circles.

This time his voice held a little more concern. "What is it?"

"Well, I didn't plan it this way. But I think we might just be getting a baby for Christmas."

Dex was up in a flash. "Are you serious? I need to get the go bag. Wait here."

She watched him rush from place to place getting what they needed for the next day or so and putting out the fire. A huge lump of emotion clogged her throat. "This is our first baby—I think we have plenty of…" She stopped midsentence when another wave of tension squeezed her belly. Okay, so that was a little closer than she expected it to be.

"Okay, don't panic, but we might want to get a move on. A Christmas baby is one thing.

A Christmas baby born in the car is something else entirely."

Even as she said it, she went over to him and stopped his frantic movements, laying her head on his chest, her belly pressed tight against him. "God, Dex. It's so perfect. So very perfect."

"What is?"

"Life," she said. Then she stretched up to receive his kiss.

* * * * *

If you enjoyed this story, check out these other great reads from Tina Beckett

Risking It All for the Children's Doc
One Hot Night with Dr. Cardoza
Miracle Baby for the Midwife
A Christmas Kiss with Her Ex-Army Doc

All available now!